Out of the corner of my eye, I saw Dean walking toward me as I stood there reading the side of a corn-starch box.

He leaned around the end of the aisle.

"You want a pop or something?"

"A pop?" I said.

"Give me a break!" Dean said. "In Chicago, they call it pop."

"Well, in Connecticut we call it free soda," I said. "And, yes, thank you."

I followed him to a cooler with a sliding top. He pulled out two cans and held them behind his back. "All right. Guess what's in each hand and you get the soda."

Before I could say anything, he leaned down and kissed me. On the lips. I held my breath the entire time. It was the first time I'd ever been kissed like that. I was stunned.

"Thank you," I blurted out.

Thank you? Had that just come out of my mouth? I completely panicked and ran out of the market.

I kept running until I got to Lane's house. I pulled open the gate and let myself in. "Lane! Lane?" I called.

"What's wrong?" she asked.

"I—I got kissed," I told her. Then I noticed the box of cornstarch in my hand. "And I shoplifted!"

Other *Gilmore Girls* Books

Coming Soon

I LOVE YOU, YOU IDIOT
I DO, DON'T I?

Gilmore girls

Like Mother, Like Daughter

ADAPTED BY CATHERINE CLARK
FROM THE TELEVISION SERIES CREATED BY
AMY SHERMAN-PALLADINO
FROM THE PILOT TELEPLAY
WRITTEN BY AMY SHERMAN-PALLADINO,
THE TELEPLAY "THE LORELAIS' FIRST DAY AT CHILTON"
WRITTEN BY AMY SHERMAN-PALLADINO,
THE TELEPLAY "KISS AND TELL"
WRITTEN BY JENJI KOHAN,
THE TELEPLAY "RORY'S DANCE"
WRITTEN BY AMY SHERMAN-PALLADINO,
AND THE TELEPLAY "FORGIVENESS AND STUFF"
WRITTEN BY JOHN STEPHENS

HarperEntertainment
An Imprint of HarperCollinsPublishers

HARPERENTERTAINMENT
An Imprint of HarperCollins*Publishers*
10 East 53rd Street
New York, New York 10022-5299

ISBN: 0-06-051023-4

First HarperEntertainment paperback printing: May 2002

Visit HarperEntertainment on the World Wide Web at
www.harpercollins.com

10   9   8   7   6   5   4   3   2   1

Gilmore girls

∽Prologue

"We mock the things we are to be." Mel Brooks said that in his two-thousand-year-old man comedy routine. You know, the one with Carl Reiner? Anyhow, it's hilarious. Buy it, listen to it, live it. That's what my mom says. My mom. She's "the thing I am to be," which, by the way if you knew my mom, is not so bad. It's pretty cool, actually.

My mom. Yes, some people think she's insane. I just say she's got energy.

My name is Lorelai Gilmore. However, since my mom is also called Lorelai Gilmore and she got here first, she has dibs on the full name so people call me Rory. And a name is not the only thing we share. We like the same music, thank God, hate the same foods (avocado, what kind of cruel joke is that?), we share some clothes, watch tons of movies, hang out, make each other laugh, basically she's my best friend. And let me tell you, it's very convenient to have your best friend living in the same house with you. I'm not sure why we're so close. Maybe it's because she had me so young. She's thirty-two. I'm sixteen. So, basically, I guess we grew up together. Now, I'd love to say that the strongest part of our bond is our mutual respect for each other, but it's not. It's our complete devotion to coffee. We're slaves to it. We talk to it. "Hey, Mr. Coffee, how are you today? Good? Glad to hear it. Me too." Mom said if she ever had a boy she'd have to name it Juan Valdez. (He's a guy in an old coffee commercial. Ask your parents, they'll know.) Anyhow, if you're like us and coffee is that important to you, then you must become acquainted with Luke's Diner. Best coffee, hands down. The man's a genius. And the crazy thing is he doesn't even like coffee. Or anything else for that matter. But no matter how crabby he acts, Mom and I go there every day. Rain, shine, snow, coffee shortages that cause the prices to shoot sky high; nothing keeps us from our daily dose of pretty brown happiness.

Yesterday morning, it was absolutely freezing. I pulled myself out of bed, piled on everything warm except the bedspread, and headed out to meet Mom at Luke's before school. It was the kind of cold where the inside of your ears hurt. I made it to Luke's, dragged myself and the thirty-five pounds of wool I was wearing inside, and there was Mom at our usual table.

"Hey, it's freezing," I said as I approached her.

"What do you need? Hot tea? Coffee?" she asked with a smile.

I sat down at the table and realized what I really needed. "Lip gloss," I told her.

Mom started rooting through her giant black leather purse. Well, she calls it a purse, but it's more like a shopping bag. It's kind of nice because it means that *I* never actually have to carry anything.

"Aha!" She pulled out a lumpy clear plastic bag with things rattling around inside and sorted through it. "I have vanilla, chocolate, strawberry, and toasted marshmallow."

"Anything in there not resembling a breakfast cereal?" I asked.

"Yes." She pulled out another large makeup bag and extracted a single tube. "It has no smell, but it changes colors with your mood."

"God, Ru*Paul* doesn't need this much makeup," I commented as she handed all the lipglosses to me.

"Well, *you're* crabby," she said.

"I'm sorry. I lost my Macy Gray CD, and I need caffeine."

"I have your CD." She pulled it out of her purse.

"Thief," I said as she set it on the table.

"Sorry. And I will get you some coffee." She hopped up from the table.

While she was at the counter, I started sniffing the different lip glosses. I was putting a sample of one on my lips when this guy wearing a blue shirt and a plaid wool coat wandered over to our table. "Hey. Good morning," he said.

"Hi." I nodded at him.

"Name's Joey," he said. "On my way to Hartford. How about you?"

"Not on my way to Hartford?" I said, looking up at him.

He leaned over and put his hands on the table. "So yeah, I've never been through here before," he said.

"Ohhh, you have too," my mom said as she walked up behind him. I started to smile.

Joey turned around, completely shocked. "Oh, hi," he said awkwardly.

"Oh, *hi*. You really like my table, don't you?" she asked.

"I was just . . ." he fumbled.

"Getting to know my daughter," Mom said as she came over and stood beside my chair.

Joey's face turned this disturbing shade of pale. "Your . . ." he began, looking at me.

I smiled at him. "Are you my new daddy?"

I thought Joey was going to faint.

"Wow," Joey finally said. "You do *not* look old enough to have a daughter. No, I mean it."

Mom just kept smiling her phony smile at him.

Joey turned to me. "And you do not look like a daughter."

"That's possibly very sweet of you," Mom said. "Thanks."

"So, um . . . daughter," Joey said. He gestured to someone sitting at the counter, and a sort of goofy-looking guy with a hopeful grin on his twenty-something face turned around. "You know, I'm traveling with a friend. So . . ."

"So she's sixteen," Mom interrupted.

Joey nodded abruptly. End of discussion. He couldn't get out of Luke's fast enough. "Bye."

"Drive safe," Mom said.

And then they left. The men of our dreams. So sad. It took Mom 2.1 seconds to start imitating the look on Joey's face, a record holdout for her, then we both cracked up. And every time we looked at each other we laughed harder and couldn't stop. It got so bad Luke almost threw us out of the diner. I've got to tell you there's nothing better than sitting there laughing with my mom. (My mom is saying a pair of patent leather go-go boots, but we're ignoring her now.)

∞1

My best friend, Lane Kim, gets dressed as she's walking to school. She basically adjusts her wardrobe so that it's a little more hip. For instance, this morning, she was wearing a pink thermal T-shirt when I first saw her. Nothing wrong with it, but it wasn't Lane. So she unfolded this tie-dye T-shirt that was stuffed into her massive backpack and pulled it on over the pink shirt. Now instead of saying, "cute little innocent girl," she was saying, "Woodstock '99."

Lane's been doing this almost as long as we've been going to school together, since the first grade. "When are you going to let your parents know you listen to the evil rock music?" I asked Lane as I walked beside her, carrying her jean jacket and her backpack while she changed her shirt. "You're an American teenager, for God's sake."

Lane shook her head. "Rory, if my parents still get upset about the obscene portion size of American food, I seriously doubt I'm gonna make any inroads with Eminem."

We stopped in front of a sign advertising a "teen hayride" as Lane put her jean jacket back on. "I have to go to that," Lane said, pointing to the sign as she pulled on her coat.

"The hayride? You're kidding," I said. Our town—Stars Hollow, Connecticut—was founded in 1779 and it's incredibly quaint and has nice old architecture and cobbled sidewalks and lots of charming, old-fashioned traditions, like hayrides.

"My parents set me up with the son of a business associate. He's gonna be a doctor." Lane smiled as she said this, but I knew all these blind dates her parents kept setting up were a nightmare for her. Lane slung her backpack over her shoulder and we continued toward school.

"How old is he?" I asked her.

"Sixteen," Lane said as she pulled her shoulder-length black hair out from under the collar of her jacket.

"So, he's going to be a doctor in a hundred years," I said.

"Well, my parents like to plan ahead," she joked.

I smiled. "And you have to go on the hayride with him?"

"*And* his older brother," she said.

"Oh, now you're kidding," I said.

She shook her head. "Koreans never joke about future doctors. So, I guess you're not going, huh?" Lane asked me.

"No. I'm still fuzzy on what's fun about sitting in the cold for two hours with a bundle of sticks up your butt," I said as we walked up the stone steps into Stars Hollow High.

"Well, don't expect *me* to clear it up for you," Lane said.

We headed for our lockers, then I went to my first

class, American lit. "For those of you who have not finished the final chapters of *Huckleberry Finn*, you may use
this time to do so," Mrs. Traister said. "For those who
have, you may start your essay now. Whichever task you
choose, do it silently."

Naturally, I started working on my paper.

The three girls who sit in front of me started putting
on nail polish.

Hey, we all have our priorities.

I want to get into Harvard. They want to get into a
dance club near Harvard.

After a few minutes, I could feel them all staring at me,
but I kept writing.

"Maybe it's a love letter," one girl whispered.

"Or her diary," another said.

"Could be a slam book," the girl in front of me added.

Sophie Larson, who sits next to me, actually got out of
her chair a little so she could look over at my notebook.
"It's the *assignment*," she said in a semidisgusted tone.

They stared at me for a second, then they turned
around and went back to their nail polish.

I smiled and kept writing about Huck. I don't mind
being different. I actually sort of like it.

∽

"Was the nail polish a good color, at least?" Lane asked
as we walked up to her house after getting out of school
that afternoon.

"It had sparkles in it," I told her. "And it smelled like
bubble gum."

"Well, there's no way Mark Twain could compete with
that," Lane said as we walked through her front door.
"Mom? We're home!" she called.

The first floor of Lane's house is their very cool antique shop: Kim's Antiques. It is unbelievably crowded with furniture and lamps and glass cases of collectibles, and you feel like a rat in a maze when you walk through. Lane and her mother kept calling out trying to locate each other.

"Look, we'll meet you in the kitchen," Lane finally told her mother.

"What?" Mrs. Kim called from what sounded like deep inside an oak wardrobe.

"The kitchen!" I said more loudly.

"Who's that?" Mrs. Kim asked.

"It's Rory, Mom," Lane called to her.

This deflated and unexcited "Oh" came back to us.

Mrs. Kim is never going to like me. "Wow, I could hear the disappointment from here," I said.

"Come on, stop it," Lane said.

I ducked to avoid a hanging chandelier. "It sucks that after all these years your mom still hates me."

"She doesn't hate you," Lane said.

"She hates my mother," I reminded her.

"She doesn't trust unmarried women," she replied.

"*You're* unmarried," I pointed out.

"I'm hayriding with a future proctologist. *I* have potential," Lane said as we rounded the corner into the kitchen.

"Go upstairs," Mrs. Kim said when she saw us. She's not the warmest person in the world when I'm around, and she's pretty strict and traditional. It's hard for me not to feel bad for Lane sometimes. Besides hiding her clothes from her mom, she has to store her CDs under the floorboards in her bedroom.

"Tea is ready," Mrs. Kim said. "I have muffins. Very healthy. No dairy, no sugar, no wheat. You have to soak them in the tea to make them soft enough to bite, but very healthy."

I smiled faintly.

"So. How was school?" Mrs. Kim asked. "None of the girls get pregnant? Drop out?"

"Not that we know of," Lane told her.

"Although come to think of it, Joanna Posner *was* glowing a little," I said.

"What?" Mrs. Kim's eyes widened. This would be her worst nightmare.

"Nothing, Momma. She's just kidding," Lane said softly.

"Boys don't like funny girls," Mrs. Kim said, glaring at me and stabbing her index finger in the air with every word.

"Noted," I said simply. Fortunately, a customer entered the store just then, so that was the end of our discussion.

"Have the muffins. Made with sprouted wheat. Only good twenty-four hours," Mrs. Kim said. "Everything's half off!" she yelled as she rushed past us to find the customer. Lane and I looked at each other. We both agreed a long time ago that it's nice to have a best friend who understands how crazy your family is, yet doesn't feel the need to constantly point it out.

∽

After school the next day, I went to meet Mom at work at the Independence Inn. We actually used to live on the property in the potting shed. The building is absolutely incredible, very classic, very Connecticut Country with tall white columns and a wraparound porch. Mom loves her job—she really makes the place function, on every level.

As I walked past the front desk, the concierge, Michel Gerard, gave me the evil eye. Why shouldn't he? He gives it to everyone. Even the guests. He's actually really good at his job and is probably not a bad person when you get past his snotty accent and his attitude. I decided not to ask Michel where Mom might be. He was obviously still mad at me for asking him to proofread my French paper the day before. As if it would take him more than five minutes. He's French.

"Mom?" I called out as I walked toward the kitchen.

"Here! She's in here!" Sookie St. James yelled through the closed door. Sookie is the inn's chef, and one of my mom's best friends. In fact, Mom and Sookie hope to open their own inn together someday. She's a really great person, an incredible chef, and a bit of a klutz, not that that's a bad thing, it's just that she tends to injure herself a lot. Luckily, the rest of the kitchen staff takes care of things before there are ever any true disasters.

I walked into the kitchen to see Mom and Sookie smiling broadly. "You're happy," I said.

Mom kept smiling. Her eyes were literally shining. "Yeah."

"Did you do something slutty?" I asked.

"I'm not *that* happy," she said. She and Sookie started giggling. Then Mom held out a plastic purple gift bag to me. "Here."

I took the bag and started smiling, too. I love getting presents—especially from Mom, because they're usually good ones.

"What's going on?" I asked. I had no clue what this was all about, but they both looked so happy that it had to be something big.

"Open it!" Mom urged me.

I reached in, rifled through the tissue paper, and

pulled out a blue-and-white plaid skirt. Sort of woolly. Lots of pleats. I had to ask. "I'm gonna be in a Britney Spears video?"

"You're going to Chilton!" Sookie blurted excitedly. She turned quickly to Mom. "Sorry."

Chilton? The most exclusive private school around? The place that practically had a shuttle bus leaving for Ivy League schools on graduation day? I couldn't believe it. How . . . when? "Mom?" I asked.

She held up a letter. "You did it, babe. You got in!" She had this huge smile on her face. I don't know if I'd ever seen her so happy.

"How did this *happen*?" I asked excitedly. "You didn't . . . with the principal, did you?"

"Oh, honey, that was a joke," Mom said with a wave of her hand. "They have an open spot and you're starting on Monday," she told me.

"Really?" I still couldn't believe it. Me, at Chilton Preparatory School? It sounded so formal, so grand, so . . . pre-Harvard.

"Really," Mom said.

"I don't believe this. Oh my God! I'm going to Chilton!" I said. I hugged Mom quickly. "Sookie, I'm going to Chilton!" I cried, hugging her too.

"I'll make oatmeal cookies," Sookie said, giggling. We were all laughing and couldn't stop. "Protestants, they love oatmeal!" Sookie said.

"I have to call Lane." I turned and started to run out of the room. Then I thought, *Am I crazy?* I turned around and raced back to Mom to hug her again. This was such incredible news. "I love you!" I said.

"Ohhh. I love *you*," she said.

I ran out of the kitchen to the lobby. Michel glared at me as I reached for the telephone.

"This is the house phone. This is not for girls calling their girls . . . friends," Michel said.

"I got into Chilton," I told him, excitedly.

He wasn't impressed.

I held up the skirt. "Chilton. It's a very exclusive private school," I said. "Hardly anyone gets in."

"Is it a boarding school?"

"No," I told him.

"Oh." He sounded disappointed. "Well, is it far away?"

"Half an hour," I told him.

"Good. Maybe you will miss the bus home sometimes," he said.

He's so pleasant. Really.

∾2

The next night, Mom and Sookie were sitting outside on the front porch talking when I came out of the house to model my Chilton uniform. I still had to buy the required blazer, shirt-blouse item, saddle shoes, and tie thing-y. "So, what do you think?" I asked.

"Wow. It makes you look smart," Sookie said.

I looked at her for a second. She was leaning against the porch railing and her face was especially pink. "Okay, no more wine for you," I told Sookie. "Mom?"

"You look like you were swallowed by a kilt," she joked.

"Okay—you can hem it," I said hesitantly.

Mom got all excited and started clapping her hands. "A little," I told her. "Only a little."

"Okay," she said as we headed inside, Sookie going toward the kitchen. My mom's an excellent seamstress and can make, hem, or install a zipper in just about anything.

"I can't believe Friday is my last day at Stars Hollow High," I said.

"I *know*," Mom said, sounding like she couldn't believe it either.

"I was so excited today, I actually dressed for gym," I told her.

"Ah! You're kidding," she said.

It was out of character for me. "*And* I played volleyball," I said.

"With other people?" she asked, as she grabbed a pincushion from a table in the living room while I moved the ottoman over so I could stand on it.

"And I learned that all this time I was avoiding group sports?" I said.

"Yeah?" Mom started to pin the kilt at about knee-level.

"Was *very* smart because I suck at them," I said.

"Well, you got that from me," she said, smiling.

"So, where's the pâté?" Sookie called as she walked back from the kitchen.

"At Zsa Zsa Gabor's house?" Mom guessed.

"Right," Sookie said. "I'm walking to the store because you have *nothing*. Do you like duck?" she asked.

"If it's made with chicken, definitely," Mom said.

"I'll be back!" Sookie called over her shoulder.

"Bye!" Mom pinned the skirt's hem for another minute, then said, "All right, this should give you an idea. Go see how you like it."

"Okay." I hopped off the ottoman and headed for my bedroom. On the way, I turned around and grabbed the banister at the bottom of the stairs. "I love being a private school girl!" I said.

Mom smiled when I said that, but she looked sort of nervous. I figured she was probably just concerned about the sewing job looming ahead of her.

I stood in front of the mirror in my bedroom and

stared at my image. I couldn't wait to start my new
school.

⋘

"And we get to wear uniforms," I told Lane as she helped
me clean out my locker on Thursday afternoon. I pulled
the last of the books off the top shelf and that was it. The
box was now completely full. "No more having people
check you out to see what jeans you're wearing, because
everyone's dressed alike and just there to learn," I explained.

"Okay, there's academic-minded, and then there's
Amish," Lane said. We started walking down the hall toward the school's front doors.

I smiled at her. "Funny."

"Thank you," she replied. "So I told my mom you're
changing schools."

"Was she thrilled?" I asked.

"The party's on Friday." Lane laughed. "Oh, I have to
go. *I* have to have a prehayride cup of tea with a future
doctor. How do I look? Korean?"

"The spitting image," I said, smiling.

"Good." She tapped my giant box. "Bye."

"Bye!" I said. When I turned to watch her go, a couple
of things fell off the top of my box. I crouched down, set
the box on the floor, and picked up a few crumpled
pieces of yellow legal paper and a book.

All of a sudden, there was this pair of legs right in
front of me, startling me. "God! You're like Ruth Gor-
don just standing there with the tannis root. Make a
noise."

"*Rosemary's Baby,*" this deep voice above me said.

I gazed up the legs. They were connected to a very good-looking boy's face. He was tall, at least six feet, and had brown hair that flopped nicely. He was wearing a leather jacket and was really, really handsome. I was completely stunned that he got the *Rosemary's Baby* reference. No one ever gets it. "Yeah," I said, standing up.

"It's a great movie," he said with this half smile. "You've got good taste." He looked at all the stuff I was trying unsuccessfully to carry. "Are you moving?"

"No, just my books are," I said.

"My family just moved here. From Chicago," he explained.

"Chicago," I repeated. He was a city boy. "Windy. Oprah."

"Yeah, that's the place," he said.

I stared at the linoleum. I didn't know what else to say. Suddenly, he leaned down and said, "I'm Dean."

"Hi," I said.

He raised his eyebrows, as if to say, Isn't there more? Aren't you forgetting something? But I'd never met a Dean before and I was momentarily stunned.

"Oh. Rory. Me. That's . . . that's me."

"Rory," he repeated.

"Well, Lorelai technically," I said.

"Lorelai. I like that," he said, still smiling.

"It's my mother's name too," I said. "She named me after herself. She was lying in the hospital thinking about how men name boys after themselves all the time, you know? So why couldn't women? She says her feminism just sort of took over. Although personally? I think a lot of Demerol also went into that decision." I stopped myself

and looked up at him. "I never talk this much." And yet, I
was. It defied logic.

We stood there for another few seconds without saying anything. "Well, I'd better go," he said.

"Oh. Sure," I said, very nonchalant. Who *wouldn't*
have to go, after that speech?

"I have to go look for a job," he said.

"Okay, good," I said. He walked past me toward the exit.
"You should check with Miss Patty," I blurted out.

"What?" He turned around too, facing me.

"About the job. You should check with Miss Patty," I
said. "She teaches dance. She was actually on Broadway
once," I explained.

He looked confused. "I . . . I don't really dance much."

"No!" I said. "She just kind of knows everything that's
going on in town. She'll know if someone's looking."

"Oh. Great." He smiled, looking sort of embarrassed.
"Thanks."

I looked down again. I was doing that a lot around
him.

He walked back toward me. "Hey, what are you doing
now?" he asked.

"Nothing. Much." I held up the crumpled pieces of
yellow legal paper. "I should throw this away at some
point."

"Well, maybe you could show me where this Miss
Patty's place is?" Dean asked.

"Yeah, I guess so. I really don't have anything important to do . . . let's go!" I said.

Dean picked up my giant box of books and papers and
we walked out of school together. It was a gorgeous fall
afternoon. "So, have you lived here all your life?" Dean
asked as we crossed the lawn in front of school.

"Yes. Well, pretty much," I said. "I was actually born in Hartford."

"That's not far," Dean said.

"Thirty minutes with no traffic," I said.

"Really?" He seemed genuinely interested, which was amazing, considering I was telling him travel times.

"I've timed it," I said.

"Okay, then." He smiled and we kept walking.

"So, do you like cake?" I asked. We were walking through town and we were going past the town's bakery.

"What?" Dean asked.

"They make really good cakes. Here," I said. "They're very . . . round." What was I talking about? Maybe I shouldn't be talking right now. My mouth was completely unreliable; it couldn't be trusted anymore.

Dean laughed. "Okay. I'll remember that." He was being very polite, considering that I sounded crazy.

"Yes. Good. Make a note," I said. "You wouldn't want to forget where the round cakes are."

It was very quiet for a few seconds. Then Dean said, "So, how are you liking *Moby Dick*?"

"Oh, it's really good," I said. I was so relieved to be done with the cake topic.

"Yeah?" Dean asked.

I smiled. "Yeah, it's my first Melville."

"Cool," Dean said.

"I mean, I know it's kind of clichéd to pick *Moby Dick* as your first Melville, but—" I stopped walking. "Hey, how did you know I was reading *Moby Dick*?" I asked.

Dean turned to face me. He looked a little uncomfortable. "Ah. Well, I've been watching you."

What? "Watching me?" I asked.

"I mean, not in a creepy 'I'm watching you' sort of way," he said. "I just . . . I've just noticed you."

"*Me*?" I couldn't believe it.

"Yeah," he admitted.

"When?" I asked.

Dean sighed. "Every day. After school, you come out and you sit under that tree there and you read. Last week it was *Madame Bovary*. This week it's *Moby Dick*."

I still didn't get it. "But why would you—"

"Because you're nice to look at," he said.

I couldn't believe he could just stand there and say that without being embarrassed.

"And because you've got unbelievable concentration."

"What?"

"Last Friday, two guys were tossing around a ball and one guy nailed the other right in the face. It was a mess," Dean said. "Blood everywhere. The nurse came out, the place was in chaos, his girlfriend was all freaking out, and you just sat there and *read*. I mean, you never even looked up. I thought, I have never seen anyone read so intensely before in my entire life. I *have* to meet that girl."

I nervously clutched the crumpled paper in my hand. This whole concept of being watched by Dean was kind of exciting and great, but it was something I had to get used to. "Maybe I didn't look up because I'm unbelievably self-centered," I told him.

"Maybe." He paused. "But I doubt it." He looked right into my eyes and smiled.

I couldn't take the intense eye contact. I looked away. We *had* to talk about something else. "So . . . did I ask you if you liked cake?" I started walking down the street again.

"Yeah, you did." Dean fell into step beside me.

"Oh. 'Cause they have really good cake there," I said.

Dean just laughed.

He was smart, funny, and very, very cute.

∽3

"So, you were late getting home tonight," Mom said. We were sitting at Luke's, picking at our side salads, waiting for our cheeseburgers to come.

"Yeah. I went to the library," I said, preoccupied, thinking about Chilton and Dean and how Dean wouldn't be at Chilton.

"Oh." Mom sounded distracted too. She took a sip of coffee and said, "Oh, I forgot to tell you, we're having dinner with the grandparents tomorrow night."

"We are?" I asked, surprised. My grandparents, Emily and Richard Gilmore. Even though they only live half an hour away in Hartford, we don't see them often. I was surprised by my mom's statement.

"Mm hmm," Mom said.

"But it's September," I said.

"So?" she asked.

"So what holiday's in September?" I asked. We usually only went to Grandma and Grandpa's for holidays. Major holidays.

"Look, it's not a holiday thing," Mom said, getting irritated. "It's just dinner, okay?"

"Fine," I said. "Sorry!" What was she so stressed about?

Luke came over to the table with our meals. "Red meat can kill you," he said as he set our burgers on the table in front of us. "Enjoy."

"So, I finished hemming your skirt today," Mom said lightly, as Luke went back to the counter.

I didn't say anything. I was still thinking about Dean. What if he found someone else to watch read *Moby Dick* outside Stars Hollow High?

Mom cleared her throat. "A grunt of acknowledgment might be nice," she said, interrupting my thoughts.

"I don't understand why we're going to dinner tomorrow night. I mean, what if I had plans? You didn't even ask me."

"If you had plans, I would've known," Mom said.

"How?" I asked.

"You would've told me," she said.

"I don't tell you everything. I have my own things," I said, crabby.

"Fine"—she shrugged—"you have things."

"That's right. I have things," I repeated.

Mom stared at me. "Hey, I had dibs on being the bitch tonight."

"Just tonight?" I mumbled.

Now she was really pissed at me. "What the hell is wrong with you?" she asked.

"I'm not sure I want to go to Chilton," I said.

"What?" She was totally stunned.

"The timing is just really bad," I said.

"The *timing* is bad?"

"And the bus ride to and from Hartford? It's like thirty minutes each way," I pointed out.

She shook her head. "I can't believe what I'm hearing."

"Plus, I don't think we should be spending that money right now," I said. "I mean, I know Chilton's got to be costing you a lot."

"Oh, you have *no* idea," she said.

"All of your money should be going toward buying an inn with Sookie," I said. See, I was thinking of both of us. I'd get to stay at Stars Hollow High with Dean, and she'd get to buy her inn.

"What about college?" she asked, really confused now. "What about Harvard?"

"We don't know that I can't get into Harvard if I stay where I am," I said.

"Okay, enough. Enough of the crazy talk!" she said. "I appreciate your concern, but I have this covered."

"I still don't want to go," I said.

"Why?" she asked.

"Because I don't!" I said. Because I just met this incredible guy and he doesn't *go* to Chilton.

"I—I have to get out of here." Mom pushed back her chair. She was completely freaking out. She grabbed her coat and rushed for the door.

"We have to *pay* first," I said.

She came back and threw a couple of bills on the table. I grabbed my coat and followed her. We don't fight or argue like this—ever. This Chilton thing was bringing out the worst in both of us.

Suddenly, I heard wooden wheels rattling on the pavement. As we crossed the street toward Miss Patty's School of Ballet, the horse-drawn teen hayride went by. I smiled at Lane, who was sitting on the back end of the horse-drawn cart, sandwiched between her two dates. I guess that technically one boy was her date and the other was his older brother. One guy was wearing a beige toggle coat, and the other one was wearing a beige trench coat. It was all very beige. Neither one of them was talking to Lane when they went past us, and they all looked completely miserable, kind of like how I felt.

We reached Miss Patty's, and her studio doors were wide open as she taught an evening ballet class for what looked like six-year-old girls. "One-two-three, one-two-three," she said. "It's a waltz, ladies."

"Oh, Rory!" Miss Patty said, her face lighting up when she saw me. "Good. I think I found a job for your male friend."

"What male friend?" Mom asked immediately.

"They need a stock boy at the supermarket," Miss Patty said. "I already talked to Taylor Doose about him. You just send him around tomorrow," she said to me. Then she took a drag of her cigarette.

"Okay," I said weakly. "Thanks."

"*What* male friend?" Mom asked again.

"Oh, he's very cute. You have good taste," Miss Patty said and she smiled at me. Then she happily went back to her miniature ballerinas, saying, "Hands in the air, not in the nose. One-two-three, one-two-three."

I started walking home before Mom had a chance to move. If I walked fast enough, maybe I could avoid the questions.

But Mom was right on my heels. "Oh, you're going to have to walk a lot faster than that. You're going to have to turn into friggin' Flo Jo to get away from me!" she called after me.

I got through the front door of our house and slammed it behind me. But Mom was right there, opening it again.

"This is about a boy," she said, slamming the door behind her, too. "Of course. I can't believe I didn't see it. All this talk about money and bus rides. You've got a thing going with a guy and you don't want to leave school."

I shoved all the books and notebooks I'd left on the sofa into my backpack. "I'm going to bed," I said. I did not want to have this discussion.

"God, I'm so dense," Mom went on. "That should've been my first thought. After all, you're *me*."

"I'm *not* you!" I said, turning around and trying to walk past her to my bedroom.

"Really. Someone willing to throw important life experiences out the window to be with a guy?" Mom said. "It *sounds* like me to me."

"Whatever," I said. I finally got around her and headed for my bedroom.

"So who is he?" she asked, following me.

"There's no guy," I said.

"Dark hair? Romantic eyes? Looks a little dangerous?" she said.

"This conversation is over," I said.

"Tattoos are good too!" she called after me.

I turned around in the hallway. "I don't want to change schools because of all the reasons I've already told you a thousand times. If you don't want to believe me, that's fine. Good night."

"Does he have a motorcycle?" Mom yelled. "Because if you're going to throw your life away, he'd better have a motorcycle!"

I went into my room and closed the door. I did not want to talk about this. Meeting Dean was this surprising and exciting thing. Now all of a sudden Mom was talking about him like he was an evil gang member, trying to lure me into his lair. A few minutes later, as I was getting ready for bed, my bedroom door opened. "I think that went pretty well, don't you?" Mom asked, coming in.

"Thanks for the knock," I said, throwing my sweater onto my bed.

"Listen, can we just start all over?" she asked. "Okay? You tell me all about the guy, and I promise not to let my head explode."

I sat on my bed and started to unlace my boots, saying nothing.

"Rory, please talk to me?" she said, sitting at the end of the bed. I didn't want to talk to her. "Okay. I'll talk. Listen, don't get me wrong. Guys are great. I'm a huge fan of guys. You don't get knocked up at sixteen being indifferent to guys," she said. "But babe, guys are always going to be there, you know? This school *isn't*. It's more important. It has to be more important."

I picked up *Moby Dick*. "I'm going to sleep," I told her.

"Rory." Mom moved closer to me. "You've always been the sensible one in this house, huh? I need you to remember that feeling now. You will kick your own butt later if you blow this."

I put down the book. "Well, it's my butt." I put my head on my pillows, turning away from her.

"Good comeback," she said.

"Thank you."

"You're welcome." She paused for a second. "Rory . . . come on . . ." she pleaded.

"I don't want to talk about this!" I said, frustrated. "Will you please, please just leave me alone?"

"Okay. Fine." She stood up. "You know, we've always had a democracy in this house. We never did anything unless we both agreed. But now I guess I'm going to have to play the mom card." She took a deep breath and said, "You are going to Chilton, whether you want to or not. Monday morning, you will be there. End of story."

"We'll see!" I said, tears filling my eyes.

"Yeah, we will!" She left the room, closing the door with a bang.

I was so angry. We never fought and I wasn't used to how bad it felt to have her mad at me. But I couldn't stop thinking about Dean and how my transferring to Chilton was going to ruin everything that could maybe, possibly happen between us.

I reached up and turned on the radio so that I'd stop thinking for a while. The Macy Gray song that Mom and I both loved was playing, which only made me feel even worse. Things had gotten really weird in the last twenty-four hours. I was starting to wish I'd never gotten into Chilton. If I hadn't, none of this would be happening.

∽4

"So. Do we go in, or do we just stand here reenacting 'The Little Match Girl'?" I asked Mom as we stood outside my grandparents' house on Friday night. We'd been standing there for a couple of minutes without ringing the doorbell. It's a very large, very imposing house. There are multiple stone fountains out front, as well as a pair of lion sculptures guarding the front door. It's more like a small, private museum than a house.

We had driven the entire way to my grandparents' house without talking—it seemed like the longest thirty minutes ever. We had barely spoken at the inn that afternoon either. It was completely unnatural for us to not talk. We both *love* to talk. It's what we do.

"Okay, look," Mom said. "I know you and me are having a thing here, and I know you hate me. But I need you to be civil, at least through dinner. Then on the way home you can pull a Menendez. Deal?"

"Fine," I said.

Mom finally stepped up and rang the doorbell. Seconds

later my grandmother opened the heavy oak door with a smile on her face. My grandmother looked perfect. She's always wearing an actual outfit, like a suit, and her hair is done, and she has on pumps with heels, and pantyhose. She'd be ready if the president dropped by in the middle of the night, *and* she'd have tea. She's very impressive that way.

"Hi, Grandma!" I said, smiling.

"Well, you're right on time," she said.

"Yeah. Yeah. No traffic at all," Mom said as we walked through the door.

"I can't tell you what a treat it is to have you girls here." Grandma took our coats.

"Oh, well. We're excited too," Mom said.

Grandma glanced at the paper coffee cup that Mom was clutching. "Is that a collector's cup, or can I throw it away for you?" she asked.

"Oh." Mom looked around, then started to toss the cup in the wastebasket by the door.

"In the kitchen, please," Grandma said.

"Oh—sorry," Mom said. It was weird, the way they communicated sometimes. Like Mom was ten or something, and constantly getting in trouble for misbehaving.

Grandma put her arm around me and we walked toward the living room. "So, I want to hear all about Chilton!" she said excitedly.

"Well, I haven't actually started yet," I told her. I still wasn't sure that I was going to. We walked into the living room, which is extremely fancy, with a crystal chandelier and antique furniture that costs more than our entire house. "Richard, look who's here!" Grandma said.

My grandfather was sitting on one of the sofas, reading a newspaper. He slid his reading glasses down his nose to get a better look at me. "Rory!" he said. "You're tall." He was wearing wool slacks, an Oxford cloth shirt, a cardigan sweater, and a bow tie—his standard outfit when he wasn't wearing a suit. He's quite tall himself, so I guess he keeps track of inches and centimeters.

"I guess," I said with a shrug.

"What's your height?" he asked.

"Five seven?" I guessed. I hadn't actually been measured in a while.

"That's tall," he said, as if I'd achieved something. He turned his head to tell my grandmother, who was fixing drinks at the table behind the sofa. "She's *tall*."

"Hi, Dad!" Mom said as she walked into the living room.

"Lorelai. Your daughter's tall," Grandpa said to her.

"Oh, I know. It's freakish," Mom replied. "We're thinking of having her studied at MIT."

Grandpa looked at her as if she were crazy, while I suppressed a smile. "Ah," he said. Then he went back to his newspaper.

"Champagne, anyone?" my grandmother offered. She came over to us, carrying a sterling silver tray with four filled crystal champagne flutes on it. It's sort of like being in an alternate universe when we're over there—their life is so different from ours.

"Oh. That's fancy," Mom said as she took a glass. I took one too.

"Well, it's not every day that I have my girls here for dinner on a day the banks are open," Grandma said.

One thing you have to give my grandmother credit for is that she's very witty. I guess that's where Mom gets it.

But as far as Grandma's joke about banks being open was concerned, I *was* still wondering why we were here

on a regular Friday night. Was this supposed to be a cel-
ebration for my going to Chilton? If so, why hadn't Mom
told me that?

"A toast." Grandma lifted her glass. "To Rory entering
Chilton. And an exciting new phase in her life!" She
smiled and then took a sip of champagne.

"Here, here," my grandfather said in agreement, not
looking up. He's obsessed with the financial news. If he
were stranded on a desert island, he'd still find a way to
get them delivered.

As I drank to the toast, I felt my grandmother smiling
at me a little too brightly and proudly, like she was ex-
pecting something. So this *was* all about Chilton. It was
too much pressure. I didn't even want to go to Chilton,
and she was talking about it being "exciting" and "new."
Grandma, Mom, and I clinked our glasses, and I felt like
a hypocrite.

"Well, let's sit, everyone. *Sit*," Grandma said.

I sat down next to my grandfather, and my grandmother sat on the love seat facing me.

"This is just wonderful," she said. "An education is the
most important thing in the world, next to family."

"And pie," my mother added with a goofy smile.

My grandparents just stared at her. So did I. She loves
pie, but still.

"Joke," she explained as she sat down next to
Grandma. "Joke."

"Ah." My grandmother sort of nodded once, then she
turned away from Mom. They both took long drinks
from their champagne glasses.

This deafening silence descended on the living room.
It was like we'd all mutually run out of things to say at
the same exact moment. I hoped dinner would be ready
soon.

My grandfather passed a section of the financial newspaper to me and I started reading about the stock market. This was shaping up to be a very slow night.

∽

"Rory, how do you like the lamb?" my grandmother asked when we were halfway through dinner.

"It's good," I said.

There were tall white candles on the dinner table, and a floral centerpiece. A fire was blazing in the fireplace behind my grandfather's chair. "Too dry?" my grandmother asked.

I shook my head. "No, it's perfect."

"Potatoes could use a little salt, though," Mom told her.

"Excuse me?" Grandma asked.

It sounded like they were about to get into an argument over salt and potatoes, so I quickly changed the subject. "So, Grandpa, how's the insurance biz?" I asked.

He sighed and finished chewing a bite. "People die, we pay. People crash cars, we pay. People lose a foot, we pay."

"Well, at least you have your new slogan," Mom joked.

I smiled. "And how are things at the motel?" Grandpa asked Mom.

"The *inn*?" Mom corrected him. "They're great." She took another sip of wine.

"Lorelai's the executive manager now," Grandma said. "Isn't that wonderful?"

"Speaking of which, Christopher called yesterday," Grandpa said as he lifted his wine glass to his lips.

I was surprised to hear Grandpa talks to my father. *I*

only got to talk to my dad once a week or so—he moved around a lot, and he wasn't great about checking in to let us know what he was up to.

"Speaking of which? How is that a 'speaking of which'?" Mom asked. She sounded annoyed, and I could see her point. I glanced nervously at Grandpa, wondering why he was bringing this up.

"He's doing very well in California," he continued. "His Internet startup goes public next month. This could mean big things for him." He looked up the table at me. "Very talented man, your father."

"She knows," Mom said.

"He always was a smart one, that boy," Grandpa said. He smiled at me. "You must take after *him*."

Mom glared at Grandpa. "Speaking of which, I'm gonna get a Coke." Mom put her napkin on the table and stood up. "Or a knife." She headed into the kitchen.

I couldn't believe my grandfather just said that. It was really insulting of him to say I was smart because of Dad, who was never even around.

I sat there for a few seconds feeling very, very uncomfortable. I felt awful for Mom, and I knew she had to feel a lot worse. I heard her banging dishes around in the kitchen. It sounded like she was doing the dishes. I set down my fork and started to get up. "I think I'm gonna go talk to her—"

"No, I'll go." Grandma got to her feet. "You stay and keep your grandfather company."

I dutifully sat back down, waiting to see what happened. It didn't matter, though. I might as well have gone into the kitchen with Grandma, because I could hear everything she and Mom said to each other.

"Is this what it's going to be like every Friday night?"

Mom was saying. "I come over and let the two of you attack me?"

Every Friday night? What was she talking about?

"You're being very dramatic," Grandma said.

"Were you at that table just now?" Mom asked.

"Yes, I was," Grandma said, "and I think you took what your father said the wrong way."

"The wrong way? How could I have taken it the wrong way? *What* was open to interpretation?" Mom questioned loudly.

I tried not to listen.

"Why do you pounce on every single thing I say?" Mom asked.

"That's absurd. You've barely uttered a word all night," Grandma replied.

"That's not true," Mom said.

"You said 'Pie', Grandma conceded.

"Oh come on," Mom said.

"You did. All I heard you say was 'pie.'"

Then I heard Mom say, "Why would he bring up Christopher? Was that really necessary?"

"He likes Christopher," Grandma said calmly.

"Isn't that interesting?" Mom's voice was getting louder. "Because as I remember, when Christopher got me pregnant, Dad didn't like him so much!"

I felt my entire dinner just sort of clumping in my stomach. They were fighting about me now. Indirectly, but it was still me.

"Oh, well, please. You were sixteen. What were we supposed to do? Throw you a party?" Grandma said.

Mom had told me once that this was how her parents felt about the choices she'd made in her life, but it had been hard for me to believe they disapproved of them so strongly. After all, everything had worked out great, for both of us.

"We were disappointed," Grandma said. "The two of you had such bright futures."

"Yes. And by not getting married, we got to *keep* those bright futures," Mom said.

"When you get pregnant, you get married," Grandma argued, stubbornly. "A child needs a mother and a father."

I kind of wanted to go in and disagree. I love my dad, and it would be great if he wanted to live closer. But Mom and I do just fine on our own. Great, in fact. We have a better mother-daughter relationship than anyone else I know. She's my best friend.

"Mom, do you think that Christopher would have his own company right now if we had gotten married? Do you think he would be anything at all?" Mom asked.

"Yes, I do," Grandma said. "Your father would have put him in the insurance business and you'd be living a lovely life right now."

"He didn't *want* to be in the insurance business, and I *am* living a lovely life right now!" Mom said. She was furious and frustrated. I had to agree with her—our life was lovely.

"That's right," Grandma said. "Far away from us. You took that girl and completely shut us out of your life."

"You wanted to *control* me!" I heard Mom argue.

"You were still a child," Grandma replied.

"I stopped being a child the minute the strip turned pink, okay?" Mom said.

I felt my face turn red, and Grandpa cleared his throat. I think we both wanted to crawl under the table.

"I had to figure out how to live. I found a good job—"

"As a *maid*," Grandma said disparagingly. "With all your brains and talent."

"I worked my way up. I *run* the place now," Mom said. "I built a life on my own with no help from anyone."

"Yes. And think of where you would've been if you had accepted a little help. Hmm? And where Rory would have been? But no. You were always too proud to accept anything from anyone," Grandma said.

"Well, I wasn't too proud to come here to you two, begging for money for my kid's school, was I?" Mom asked.

What? That was what this was all about? I was totally shocked. I couldn't believe Mom would do something like that—she prided herself on living independently. Wow. This whole, entire fight was because of something I wanted to do. Why hadn't Mom just *told* me we couldn't afford Chilton?

"But you're too proud to let her know where you got it from, aren't you?" Grandma said. "Well, fine. You have your precious pride and I have my weekly dinners."

Weekly dinners. So it was true. Every Friday night we'd be here.

I didn't know what to do. Should I go in there and thank Grandma for giving us the money so I could go to Chilton? Should I thank Mom for asking them for the money? Should I apologize for wanting to go to Chilton in the first place?

I looked at Grandpa to see if he had a clue but I wasn't going to get an answer from him.

He had fallen asleep.

Mom and I left about ten minutes later, after pretending to eat part of a twelve-layer chocolate cake. I discovered that at my grandparents' house, it doesn't matter if people are fighting or if no one's speaking to each other, you still have dessert.

Once we got outside, Mom slumped against the stone wall, by the door. "Mom?" I said, worried. She looked very pale, like she might pass out. She hadn't eaten much of anything at dinner.

She smiled at me. "I'm okay. I just . . . do I look shorter?" she asked. " 'Cause I feel shorter."

"Hey . . . how about I buy you a cup of coffee?" I asked.

"Oh, yeah." She put her arm around my shoulders and we walked down the front steps together. "You drive, though, okay? Because I don't think my feet will reach the pedals."

As we walked toward Luke's about a half hour later, I wanted to break the ice. Much like the drive to Hartford, we hadn't really said much in the car. "So. Nice dinner at the grandparents' house," I casually said.

"Oh, yeah. Her dishes have never been cleaner," Mom said wearily.

"You and Grandma seemed to have a nice talk," I said with a smile.

She stopped before going inside Luke's. "How much did you hear?"

"Oh, not much," I said with a shrug. "You know, snippets."

"Snippets," she repeated.

"Little snippets," I said.

"So basically everything?" she asked.

"Basically, yes," I admitted.

Mom opened the door and we walked into Luke's. "Well, the best laid plans."

I took off my jacket and we sat at an empty table by the door. It was quiet at Luke's. I liked that. It was nice to have the place almost all to ourselves. "I think it was really brave of you to ask them for money," I told Mom.

"Oh. I so do not want to talk about it," she said.

"So, how many meals is it going to take until we're off the hook?" I asked, trying to put a good spin on things. Friday nights wouldn't be the same from now on—but maybe I'd finally get to know my grandparents a little better.

"I think the deli spread at my funeral will be the last one," Mom said. Then she started to smile. "Hey . . . wait . . . does that mean?" she asked.

"Can't let a perfectly good plaid skirt go to waste," I said, smiling.

"Ah, honey. You won't be sorry." She looked so happy. I realized that I hadn't seen her actually smile in a while. It was nice. She must have been pretty stressed about Chilton from the beginning, trying to figure out how to pay for the tuition. And there I was, telling her I wouldn't go. I never would have said that if I'd known what she was going through. It was so like her not to tell me, to just pull it off and make it look easy—when she was making this huge sacrifice for me.

Luke came over for our order. He was dressed up, for him, wearing a button-down shirt that wasn't made of flannel. He wasn't even wearing a baseball cap. I'd forgotten what his head looked like without a cap. Mom noticed too. "Wow," she said, "you look nice. Really nice."

"I had a meeting earlier at the bank. They like collars," he replied. "You look nice too."

"I had a flagellation to go to," Mom responded dryly. Luke smiled and took our order. "So, tell me about the guy," Mom said after Luke walked away. *Oh, God. Here it comes*, I thought. She's going to grill me about Dean now.

"You know what's really special about our relationship?" I said. "The total understanding about the need for one's privacy. I mean, you *really* understand boundaries."

"So. Tell me about the guy," she pressed.

"Mom . . ." I said.

"Is he dreamy?" she asked.

Dreamy? I rolled my eyes. "That's so Nick at Nite."

"Well, I'm going to find out anyway," she said.

"Really? How?" I asked.

"I'll spy," she said.

Luke brought two mugs of coffee and a plate of chili fries to the table. "Coffee . . . fries . . ." he said as he set them down. Then he stood there for a few seconds as we started to drink our coffee. "I can't stand it," he finally said. "This is so unhealthy. Rory, please, put down that cup of coffee. You do not want to grow up to be like your mom."

I looked at Luke, then I looked at Mom. "Sorry," I said. "Too late."

We smiled at each other. I was *so* glad our fight about Chilton was over. Mom was right. I couldn't miss this opportunity, Dean or no Dean.

"So, tell me about the guy," Mom said again, once Luke was back behind the counter.

"Check, please!" I joked.

"No really, are you embarrassed to bring him up?" she pressed.

I knew she was going to ask me about Dean for the rest of the night. But that was okay. I was going to Chilton. And my Mom made the whole thing happen.

∞5

It wasn't too long until Mom and I settled into the Friday night dinner at the grandparents' house routine.

I actually enjoyed it. It was great spending time with my grandparents, and my grandfather even took me to the club to try to teach me golf—utter failure on the sporting side, but a huge success on the bonding side. We discovered we have similar interests, and he has given me some great first editions of books I really love. Regardless, now that I was going to Chilton, I could think of other things I'd rather do on a Friday night, like hang out with Lane. Or accidentally run into Dean. I didn't get to see them as much as I wanted to. Chilton was a lot more demanding academically than my old high school, so my weekday nights were filled with homework. It was really competitive, and nobody there liked me.

Paris Geller hated me most. She'd vowed to make my life miserable—literally—after I got to Chilton and she found out I might be competing with her in our classes. Apparently when I came along, I messed up her master plan. Her friends, Madeline and Louise, hated me also. They made it a group activity.

Then there was Tristin Dugray, who got no bigger thrill out of life than making fun of me. He called me Mary for the first two weeks I went to Chilton. As in the Virgin Mary.

By the end of the school week, I was usually pretty exhausted, and going to dinner at my grandparents' house on Friday nights did have its perks. We were waited on hand and foot, the food was always delicious, and the conversation was never dull.

"So tomorrow our lawyer, Joseph Stanford, is coming by," my grandmother announced as she sipped her after-dinner coffee.

"Ugh," Mom groaned. "Crazy Sissy's dad."

"That's terrible!" Grandma said. "Sissy was a good friend of yours."

"Mom, Sissy talked to her stuffed animals and they answered her," Mom said.

"Let's just start a new topic," I said, hoping I could stave off an argument.

But Grandma wasn't ready to let it go yet. "You're impossible," she said to Mom.

"She said a *new* topic, Mom."

Grandma was getting really exasperated. "Everything's a joke. Everyone's a punch line," she said in disgust.

"Okay, I'm sorry," Mom apologized.

But Grandma wasn't through yet. "My daughter— Henny Youngman," she said.

My grandfather came back into the dining room. "Sorry for that," he said. He sat back down at the dinner table. "A little trouble in our China office. What did I miss?"

"I was being impossible, and then I turned into a Jewish comedian," Mom told him.

"Ah. Very well. Continue," Grandpa said with a smile. This didn't faze him at all. That was one of the things I really liked about him—he never got involved in Mom and Grandma's silly disagreements.

"Thank you. Where was I?" Grandma asked.

"Uh, Joseph Stanford is coming tomorrow," I reminded her.

"Yes! So, Rory, your grandfather and I thought it might be nice after dinner for you to go around the house and pick out what you'd like us to leave you in our wills." Grandma smiled at me. This was bizarre. She was talking about death and wills over dinner. Their lawyer was coming to the house tomorrow to take inventory of their lives and she wanted me to pick out the things I wanted?

"Take a look at that desk in my office," my grandfather said to me. "It's a really fine Georgian piece."

Mom was as stunned as I was by the turn of events. "Why don't I ever bring a tape recorder to these dinners?" she wondered.

"Oh, well, anything you want to leave me is fine," I said. I didn't want anything in particular—all I wanted was for my grandparents to stick around as long as possible, so they wouldn't *need* their wills.

"Nonsense!" Grandma said. "You should have what you like. So just look around and when you see something you like, stick a Post-it on it." She smiled brightly at me.

Shopping at my grandparents' house with Post-its? Making a wish list for the days they weren't here anymore? Were they insane? I was speechless.

"Okay, you two have officially hit a new level of weird that even *I* marvel at," Mom commented.

"You can pick out things too, you know," Grandma told her.

"Oh. Well, now it's way less creepy," Mom said.

"Did you hear that, Richard?" Grandma asked. "Apparently we're creepy."

"Yes, well, live and learn," my grandfather said dryly.

I looked across the table at Mom and tried not to laugh.

The maid walked into the dining room, carrying a silver tray with four crystal dishes of what looked like chocolate pudding. "Oh, cool!" I said as the maid set a dish in front of me.

"What's that?" Mom asked.

"It's dessert," Grandma said briskly.

"It's pudding," Mom said.

"Well, if you knew what it was, then why did you ask?" Grandma said.

"You don't like pudding," Mom said.

Oh my God. They were bickering about chocolate pudding. "Yes, but *you* like pudding," Grandma said.

"Oh, I love pudding. I worship it," Mom said. "I have a bowl up on the mantel at home with the Virgin Mary, a glass of wine, and a dollar bill next to it," she went on, while Grandma rolled her eyes.

"I've never had pudding from a crystal bowl before," I said in admiration. You wouldn't think it would affect the taste, but it did.

"You like the bowl? Put a Post-it on it when you're done," Grandma told me.

After we finished dinner, Mom and I wandered around the house with our pads of Post-its. My grandparents have a lot of nice things, and it was hard to choose. At first I wasn't picking anything, but Grandma insisted that I start using the Post-its or I would regret it later.

Mom and I paused beside a huge vase that looked like it must have been used for barter in a Japanese samurai battle at some point.

"So what do we think of this?" Mom asked.

"Where would we put it?" I said.

"I don't know. The Emily and Richard Gilmore Psycho Museum?" she said.

"This is the strangest evening I've ever spent here," I said, just as Grandma walked back into the living room.

"So, how are we doing?" she asked brightly.

"Great," Mom said. "Just getting ready for the big day," she joked as she ripped off a Post-it and stuck it onto the large vase.

"Very nice," Grandma said, nodding her approval.

"So, um, it's getting late, Mom. Unless you've got some funeral plots for us to decorate, we should really be going," Mom said.

"Any special requests for dinner next week?" Grandma asked, smiling at me.

"Oh, well . . ." I glanced at Mom. We'd discussed this earlier in the car. And at home. And for the past two weeks. Next Friday was my birthday, and we wanted to have a big party at our house, like we did every year. It was tradition.

"Mom, I want to talk to you for a minute," she said. "Rory, why don't you go say goodbye to Grandpa?"

"Very smooth," I said under my breath as I left the room. I went to talk to Grandpa for a few minutes, then went outside to the car with Mom.

Mom climbed into the Jeep and shut the door. "So. How would you like *two* birthday parties this year?" She looked apologetic.

"You couldn't get her to cave," I said.

"No, but she did agree to make the string quartet learn 'Like a Virgin,'" she said, smiling.

"Well, you tried," I said, a little bit disappointed.

"Sweetie, I promise—Saturday night we'll do it up right at home," she said. "A Stars Hollow extravaganza."

I know she was right. Our birthday parties were usually major town events. "So, is this party Grandma's having going to be a big deal?" I asked. I wondered what she could do to a birthday, when a Friday night dinner at their house became a formal event.

"Not really," Mom said. "The government will close that day. Flags will fly at half-mast. Barbra Streisand will give her final concert . . . again."

"Uh huh," I said.

"Now, the pope has previous plans, but he's trying to get out of them," she went on. "However, Elvis and Jim Morrison are coming, and they're bringing chips."

"You ask a simple question . . ." I said as Mom started the Jeep. She was being funny about it, but I really wanted to know what sort of party it would be.

The party at our house would be the *real* party, though. No offense to my grandparents, but Mom and I just have our own way of doing things, and we love throwing parties.

I wondered if I should invite Dean. He should be there. I wanted him to be there.

Things had been moving super slowly with him, but last week they'd shifted into higher gear. One day he'd gotten on my bus to Chilton, and sat behind me, just to say hi. I'd stopped in to see him at Doose's, and even though our conversation didn't go much beyond "Paper or plastic?" it still felt meaningful. It was like we were making these tiny little gestures toward each other.

Then last week he had come over to our neighbors, Babette and Morey's, to deliver sodas from the market for their cat Cinnamon's wake (they were very attached to this cat, okay?) and we had this awkward moment outside where he said he could see I wasn't interested in him so he would quit "bothering" me. I was so surprised I didn't know what to say. He started walking away when I blurted out that I was. Interested. So we both know we like each other. Now what? A lot of awkward silences.

I really wanted him to come to my birthday party, but I wasn't sure I was ready for that. Wouldn't it put too much pressure on both of us? Maybe I needed *three* birthday parties, one just with Dean.

On Tuesday morning I had just gotten to Chilton and was opening my locker when Tristin came up and leaned against the locker next to mine. "Hey," he said, standing a little too close to me.

"What, Tristin?" I asked, turning toward him.

"I just wanted to say happy birthday," he said.

"It's not my birthday," I told him.

He held up a white envelope. "No, but it will be." He opened the thick card that was inside the envelope and started to read. "On Friday at four-oh-three in the morning, Lorelai Leigh—"

"What is that?" I grabbed the card from him and my eyes widened as I quickly scanned it. It was a formal invitation—a formal announcement of my birthday. "Emily and Richard Gilmore were blessed with a perfect baby granddaughter, Lorelai Leigh. Please join us this Friday to celebrate this joyous occasion. Seven o'clock. Black tie optional."

"Who else got these?" I asked Tristin, horrified.

"I don't know," he said with a shrug. "Everyone in our class, I think."

Everyone in our class? An entire group of sophomores that did not know me, or even like me? I closed my locker. "I have to go." I started walking down the hall.

"I'll see you Friday, birthday girl!" Tristin yelled after me.

I kept walking, staring at the invitation in my hand. How could my grandparents do this to me? "That's her," I heard Louise say to another girl as I walked past her.

"My parents are *making* me go," her friend said.

"Another obligation party," Louise complained.

"My life stinks." Her friend sighed.

Her life stinks? I thought as I looked for a place to hide. Everyone in my class was being forced to come to my birthday party. This was a nightmare.

I'd never dreaded my birthday before.

My life now officially sucked.

6

"Wow. Nice face you got on there," Mom said in a cheery voice when I walked in to meet her at Luke's, dragging my feet, dragging my backpack, and dragging my soul.

"Coffee," I said after sitting down.

"Bad day?" Mom asked.

"I've now used the word 'sucks' so much that it's lost all meaning to me," I said.

"Well, maybe this will cheer you up," she said. She unzipped this garment bag she was holding and pulled out a hunk of gray-green tulle.

"What is *that*?" I asked.

"These are our party dresses!" she said happily.

I could not picture either one of us wearing these dresses. "So it's a Halloween party?" I said.

"Listen, you." Mom smiled. "So I'm shopping today with your grandmother, and it's a whole three hours of '*Who* are you buying that for, Mom? Have you *met* Rory?' and then finally I talked, and she listened, and she wound up getting you something I think you're really going to like."

Mom was literally beaming. She doesn't do this when she's talking about Grandma. It made me happy for her, even though I didn't feel any better. "Really?" I asked.

"Yes, really. And of course she insisted on buying us these dresses, but I think I can do something with them to make them better," Mom said.

"Wow. I've never seen you like this after spending time with Grandma," I said.

"Well, it's been a long time since we got together and didn't end up fighting. It was refreshing. It wasn't exactly fun, but I didn't get that shooting pain in my eye like I usually do," Mom joked.

"Wow. That's great," I said.

Luke came over with two giant cups of coffee for us. "So I hear you're having a party Saturday," he said.

"Yeah, Mom's famous for her blowouts," I told him.

"The best one was her eighth birthday," Mom said, looking across the table at me.

"Oh, yeah that was good," I said, nodding.

"The cops shut us down," Mom told Luke.

"The cops shut down an eight-year-old's birthday party?" Luke asked.

"*And* arrested the clown," I added. Mom and I laughed.

"I don't want to hear any more of this," Luke said as he went back to the counter.

Mom and I both sipped our coffee. "So, now tell me, why Miss Lemonhead today?" she asked. I couldn't tell Mom how upset I was about my entire Chilton class coming to the party now. She and Grandma were actually *bonding*.

"Nothing," I said. "I . . . I'm fine. I just got an A-minus

on a French test that I should have gotten an A on." Actually that wasn't a lie. A-minuses do make me crabby. I hate A-minuses. They're A's mocking you.

"Oh, honey, an A-minus is *awesome*," Mom said genuinely.

"Yeah, it's—it's fine," I said.

Mom started checking out the party dresses in the garment bag again. "Let me see. Maybe we should really embrace the whole tulle thing. Go totally modern Cinderella. What do you think?" she asked. "It's *your* birthday."

"Yeah," I said with a fake smile. "Lucky me."

∽

Friday morning at 4:03 A.M., Mom came into my room to wake me up. She kissed my cheek and said, "Happy birthday, little girl."

I struggled to wake up. "Hey," I said as Mom climbed onto the bed beside me. I wrapped my arms around her arm and snuggled close to her. We'd done this every year on my birthday for as long as I could remember. It was one of my favorite birthday traditions.

"I can't believe how fast you're growing up," Mom said softly, looking over at me.

"Really?" I asked groggily. "It feels *slow*."

"Trust me, it's fast. What do you think of your life so far?" she asked.

"I think it's pretty good," I said, my voice muffled by my pillow.

"Any complaints?" Mom asked.

"Well . . . I'd like that whole humidity thing to go away," I said.

"All right. I'll work on that," Mom said.

"So, do I look older?" I asked.

Mom turned her head to give me a closer look. "Oh, yeah. You walk into Denny's before five? You've got yourself a discount."

"Good deal." I closed my eyes and put my head on her shoulder.

"So you know what I think?" Mom said. "I think you're a great, cool kid, and the best friend a girl could have."

"Back at ya," I whispered.

"And it's so hard to believe that at exactly this time many moons ago, I was lying in exactly the same position . . ."

I took a deep breath. "Oh boy. Here we go."

"Only I had a huge, fat stomach and big fat ankles," she went on, "and I was swearing like a sailor—"

"On leave," I reminded her.

"On leave—right! And there I was—"

"In labor," I added.

"And while some have called it the most meaningful experience of your life, to me it was something more akin to doing the splits on a crate of dynamite."

"I wonder if the Waltons ever did this," I mused.

Mom continued. "And I was screaming and swearing, and being surrounded as I was by a hundred prominent doctors, I just *assumed* there was an actual use for the cup of ice chips they gave me."

"There wasn't," I said, helping.

"But pelting the nurses sure was fun!" Mom said.

I squeezed her arm and held her close. "I love you, Mom."

"Shh. I'm getting to the part where he sees your head," she said.

I settled in for the rest of the story.

∾

"You should not have to go to school today," Lane declared as we walked into Luke's before school.

"Have to," I said. "Latin test."

"Every *day* you have a test," Lane commented. "When do you have time to learn anything to be tested on?" She had a point.

"Hey, wrong table," Luke said when Lane and I tried to sit at the counter.

"Since when is there a right table?" I asked.

"Since the coffee cake I baked for you and the stupid balloons I blew up are at that table, over there." Luke pointed to the back of the diner, where five red, white, and blue balloons were tied to the napkin dispenser on a table.

"You blew up balloons for me?" I said. "Oh, Luke, you old softie."

"I count to three, it's gone," he said gruffly. I guessed this niceness and balloons thing was ruining his image.

"Thank you!" I told him. Then Lane and I hurried over to the table.

"Are you okay?" Lane asked as I sat down across from her.

"Yeah, I'm just . . . I'm getting old, Lane." I sighed and picked up my fork.

"You've been a little quiet this morning," Lane said. We stuck our forks into the coffee cake and started to eat. It was scrumptious.

"I'm just dreading this whole night," I said. "I mean, it's bad enough that I have to see these stupid kids from Chilton every day. But tonight? On my birthday? I mean,

I've never even talked to most of them. God, they're gonna think I am the biggest freak, that I need my grandma to get people to come to my party."

"Well, what did Lorelai say when you told her?" Lane asked.

"I didn't."

"Why not?"

"Because of the pudding," I told her.

Lane stared at me like I was crazy. "Oh, the pudding. Right, I forgot about the pudding," she said.

"My grandmother served us pudding the other night and then she went shopping with my mom and they didn't fight," I explained. "I don't know. I mean, they never get along, and now suddenly they're getting along, and I knew that if I told Mom about the invites, she'd wig out and call Grandma and that would be the end of the pudding."

"You know you can *buy* pudding," Lane said after a minute.

I nodded. "It's one night, right?"

"Right," Lane agreed.

"I can stand it for one night." I'd been trying to tell myself this ever since the invitations descended on Chilton en masse. What was one more night of humiliation and awkwardness, anyway—in the grand scheme of things?

The diner door opened with a jingle, and Dean walked in. He closed the door behind him and glanced around Luke's. He stopped for a second when he saw me, then went to the counter.

"Coffee to go, please," Dean told Luke.

While Luke filled a cup for him, Dean turned and looked over his shoulder at me again. I looked up and he looked away. He turned back and then this huge smile broke out across his face.

"Here you go," Luke said, handing him his coffee.

Dean thanked him, then headed for the door. Just before he left, he looked over at me again. "Happy birthday!" he mouthed, then he smiled again.

I felt my face get hot, then I looked away and smiled. I'd talked to Dean at the market a couple of nights ago and told him my birthday was coming up. He had to work Saturday night, and he'd told me he would come by the house after the party was over. We were still being a little secretive. "Why are you smiling?" Lane asked.

"Oh. I'm just thinking about pudding," I lied.

No matter what happened tonight, this could not be a bad birthday now. It just couldn't be.

∽

I glanced at my watch. 7:58 P.M. We were one hour into the party at Grandma and Grandpa's. One hour down, one hour to go. So far I'd managed to avoid the Chilton contingent, but I knew I was on borrowed time. The house looked really nice, and there was a staff of caterers bigger than my class at Chilton circulating with trays of drinks and snacks. But I'd rather just be having the usual Friday night dinner with my grandparents. Instead, the house was full of a bizarre mixture of my grandparents' friends and the Chiltonites.

"Here." Mom handed me a glass and sat down next to me.

"What is it?" I asked.

"A Shirley Temple," she said.

"What are you drinking?" I asked.

"A Shirley Temple Black." I sniffed her drink.

"Wow," I said.

"I got your Good Ship Lollipop right here, mister,"

Mom said, taking a sip. "So, do you want something to eat?"

"Everything smells funny," I said as I adjusted the heel strap on my shoe.

"Oh, *there* you are!" Grandma said as she walked up to us. She looked very elegant wearing a blue-gray suit and a simple strand of pearls around her neck. "Come, there're some people I want you to meet." She took my arm and pulled me to my feet.

Grandma must have introduced me to thirty of her friends before I was able to slip away to look for Grandpa. I finally found him busy discussing business with a bunch of men from his office. When Grandpa introduced me, they all handed me envelopes, in unison, then they went off to call someone in their office. I was about to look for Mom when Grandma found me again.

"Rory, there's a whole group of your school friends in the library!" she said excitedly. "Let's go say hello to them."

A group of *friends* from Chilton? Hardly. Grandma ushered me toward the library.

We got to the doorway and I was looking at twenty kids from Chilton, none of whom I actually knew on a first-name basis. It seemed like a really good time to bolt. "I have to go to the bathroom," I told Grandma, trying to move away.

"Just say hello first. Go on, I'll hold those for you." She took the birthday cards and gave me a gentle push. Then she took off, leaving me standing in the middle of the room.

"Who's that?" one of the guys standing by the fireplace asked when I walked a little further into the library.

"I think it's her party," the guy next to him said.

"Oh."

Then they both stood there staring at me, not saying

anything. I'd never felt so embarrassed in my life! I
turned around and walked quickly out of the room, trying to escape. That's when I saw this short girl with long,
blond hair, wearing a very expensive-looking dress. It
couldn't be. "Paris?" I said.

She turned around. "My parents made me come," she
blurted.

"Oh God," I muttered.

"Otherwise I wouldn't *be* here. You *believe* me, don't
you?" she called as I walked away.

This was unbelievable. I had to get out of there. I
headed for the front door—I could at least step out for a
few minutes and get some fresh air.

But just as I neared the front door, Tristin walked in,
complete with suit and tie. He had his hands in his pock-
ets and he looked completely relaxed and at home. "Oh,
coming to greet me?" he asked, arrogant as usual.

"Hello, Tristin," I said.

"So where's my birthday kiss?" he asked.

"It's *my* birthday," I said.

"So I'll give *you* a birthday kiss," Tristin offered as he
came closer.

"What is *wrong* with you?" I asked him.

"Okay, I gotta tell you something. I'm madly in love
with you," he said.

"Well, good luck with that," I said.

"I can't eat, I can't sleep . . . I wake up in the middle of
the night calling out your name. Rory, Rory!"

"Would you shut up, please?" I said.

"Rory, who's your friend?" Grandpa asked, walking
into the foyer just then.

"I don't know, but this is Tristin," I said, desperate to
escape.

"Excuse me?" Grandpa said.

"Tristin Dugray, sir."

"Dugray?" Grandpa reached out to shake Tristin's hand. "Are you any relation to Janlen Dugray?"

"That's my grandfather, sir," Tristin said. Suddenly he's nice and polite? He was such a phony, it made me sick.

"Well, I've done business with Janlen for *years*," Grandpa said. "He's a fine man."

"That he is," Tristin agreed.

"Well, Rory, you have very good taste in friends. I approve," Grandpa said. Then a friend of his came to call Grandpa away, so Tristin and I were alone again.

"He likes me," Tristin said cockily.

"He's *drunk*," I said.

"Come on." Tristin reached for my hand. "Let's take a walk."

I pulled back my hand. "This is *stupid*. You don't even like me! You just have this weird need to prove that I'll go out with you. That's not liking someone."

"Why are you fighting this?" Tristin asked. "You're gonna give in eventually."

"I'm going to go find my mom," I said. I started to walk back into the living room.

"Wow, meeting your mom." Tristin rubbed his hands together. "It's a bit sudden, but okay—I'm ready!" he called after me.

I could not get away from him fast enough. I couldn't get away from this *party* fast enough.

"Oh, there you are!" Grandma reached out and reeled me in, just as I went past her. "I think it's time that you said a few words to your guests."

"What?" I looked at Mom with pleading eyes.

"Just a little speech to say thank you and tell everyone

how it feels to be one year older," Grandma continued, completely oblivious to how uncomfortable I was getting.

Mom shook her head and tried to intervene. "Mom, I don't think she wants—"

"She's the hostess, Lorelai," Grandma said. "This is her responsibility."

What? "I am *not* the hostess!" I lashed out. "*You* are!"

"Hey, honey, hold on," Mom said, looking concerned.

I was so angry that my eyes were filling with tears as I looked at Grandma. "This is *your* party, and these are your guests, and I don't have anything to say to them, so *you* give the speech."

"Rory!" Grandma said, completely shocked by my outburst.

"Excuse me," I said. Then I ran upstairs to Mom's old room and slammed the door behind me.

7

"Hey. Can I come in?" Mom peeked her head through the door a few minutes later. I was lying on the bed contemplating the ceiling, and thinking about what an awful granddaughter I was. I was ungrateful. Very possibly rude. Unappreciative too.

I'd just felt so *trapped* down there. Grandma didn't understand that what might come naturally to her was impossible for me.

"It's your room," I said to Mom as she walked in.

"How are you doing?" she asked, coming over to the bed.

"I'm sorry I snapped at Grandma," I said, sitting up.

"Yeah, huh?" She sat down on the edge of the bed. "That was a pretty *Freaky Friday* moment we had back there."

"She just went ahead and invited all those kids from Chilton," I told her.

"You're kidding! I thought she checked on that with you." Mom rubbed my leg to comfort me.

"She didn't ask me or tell me," I said.

"Oh, man, I'm so sorry!" Mom said.

"It just—I don't know, but it *really* made me mad."

"Honey, why didn't you tell me?" Mom asked.

"Because you were happy," I explained. "I mean, it's not very often that there's peace between you two. I didn't want to screw everything up."

"Rory, I appreciate you wanting Mom and me to get along, but you shouldn't keep stuff like that from me," Mom said.

"I feel terrible," I said. "I mean, I've never yelled at her before."

"Listen, you'll apologize, all will be forgotten," Mom said. "You'll see." She got up and started wandering around her ex-bedroom, examining the posters, the curtains, the dresser, everything that hadn't been touched since she had moved out. "Man. It's like time has stood still in this room."

"It must be weird for you to be in this room now," I said.

"Yeah, it was weird for me to be in this room *then*."

I nodded. "I now officially know what it feels like to have grown up here."

"It's not official until you're huddled in a corner eating your hair," she said.

"Do you remember your last birthday here?" I asked.

"Yeah. We had just had a fight, and I was lying on the bed, just like you are now."

"What did you fight about?" I asked. Had Grandma embarrassed her too?

"Oh." Mom sat on the bed, then leaned back against the headboard. I leaned next to her, against a pile of pillows. "Well, I was pregnant," she said.

"Oh, that."

"And I said something at the table about the pâté

smelling like Clorox, and one thing led to another and I wound up here. I hadn't told anybody yet about me. And you." She turned to me and smiled.

"That must have been really hard on you," I said.

She nodded. "Yeah. I remember when I finally told them, it was the only time they ever looked small to me."

I really could not imagine how hard telling them must have been, especially now that I knew my grandparents a little bit better. "I guess I'd better go find Grandma," I said.

"Mm. Give her a minute—"

Grandma appeared in the doorway. "*There* you are!"

"She'll find us," Mom said, completing her thought.

"You are both being very rude," Grandma said as she walked into the room. She didn't look happy. "This isn't my birthday party, you know."

Mom sat up on the bed. "Sorry, Mom."

"Honestly, the way the two of you act," Grandma said.

"Grandma, I just want to—" I started to say.

"We'll talk about this later," she said curtly, interrupting me. "Now go."

Mom and I climbed off the bed and walked past her. It felt like we were two girls who'd just gotten in trouble together. I hated that I'd made Grandma feel bad, or that I'd embarrassed her. But she really pushed me to it.

I didn't want to go back downstairs, but I knew I had no choice. At least Mom was with me.

◊

When we tried to say goodbye to her at the end of the night, Grandma was still icy with me—with both of us.

"Hey, Mom. Great party," Mom told her. "One of your best. I even liked those brown mushroom things."

My grandmother didn't even fake a smile.

"Grandma, can I talk to you for a sec?" I asked timidly.

She wouldn't make eye contact with me. "Richard, the girls are leaving!" she called to my grandfather. Then she walked past me without even acknowledging my question.

"Well, Rory, I hope you had a good time," my grandfather said as he came up to us.

"Yeah. I did," I said.

"Now, I know that your grandmother has already bought you a gift and signed my name to it. That was part of our agreement when we got married." He smiled. "However, I feel this occasion calls for something a little extra." He handed me a white envelope. "Put that toward your trip to Fez."

"Oh, Grandpa!" I said.

"You're a good girl, Rory. Happy birthday," he said warmly.

"I don't deserve this," I said, looking at the envelope he'd given me.

"Fine, hand it over then," Mom told me.

Grandma paused in front of us as she carried some dirty glasses to the kitchen. "You girls should get going. You've got quite a drive ahead of you." But I didn't want to leave right away, because I didn't want the night to end like this—no matter how bad the party had been, my grandmother had done it all for me.

"Grandma, we're having a party tomorrow at our house," I said. "I mean, it won't be anything like this, but it will be fun, and maybe you and Grandpa can come?" I asked her.

"Why, that's very sweet, dear, but I'm afraid we already have plans," she said. Her tone made it clear that she wasn't interested. She was still too mad at me.

"Oh." She'd never talked to me like that before. I felt like crying. "Oh—okay," I stammered.

"Have a safe trip," she said, as if we were total strangers.

I felt so awful about everything. It was hard to believe this was how I'd celebrated my birthday. My grandmother hated me now.

I had to make it up to her somehow. I wanted to, desperately. But how, when she wouldn't even talk to me?

∞

The next morning, I got up early and drove to Chilton to attend the college fair. Sookie and my mom were already getting stuff ready for the birthday party that night. I kept trying not to think about what a disaster the party the night before had been as I drove to Chilton—and about how much I'd disappointed my grandmother too. I hoped I wouldn't run into anyone who had been at my party. And if I did? I hoped they wouldn't mention it.

I parked the Jeep and wandered along the row of tables and booths with representatives from different colleges and universities. My heart skipped when I saw the Harvard table ahead of me.

"New brochure?" I asked the Harvard representative. I didn't recognize the photograph on the cover of this one.

"Yes." She handed me a catalog, and I smiled. I was just digging into it when Paris walked up and stood right in front of me.

"What are you doing here?" she demanded.

"There's a college fair going on," I said.

"No. I mean, what are you doing *here*?" Paris pointed to the Harvard table.

"I'm getting a new brochure," I said.

"Why?" She kept glaring at me.

"Because they're not selling pizza," I said. Then I figured it out. Her, me, Harvard. "Oh no," I groaned.

"You can't," she told me.

Paris was one of the smartest people in our class, if not the smartest. She knew the answer to everything. When I met her, the first thing she told me was that she would be editor of the school paper and also valedictorian when we graduated. She even said that I would never catch up and would never be able to beat her.

"You're applying to Harvard?" I asked. I did not want to see her on another school campus as long as I lived. She had sworn to make my life a living hell once. And so far she was succeeding.

"Yes," she said.

"No!" This couldn't be happening.

"Ten generations of Gellers have gone to Harvard," she explained. "I *have* to go to Harvard."

"I can't believe this," I said.

"You can go somewhere else," Paris told me, as if she were my guidance counselor. "Go to Brandeis. Brandeis is nice."

She didn't understand. "I've only ever wanted to go to Harvard. That's it! Nowhere else." We both stood there and looked at each other for a few seconds. It was a showdown. Nobody was giving in. A couple of centuries ago, if we'd been men, rich men, we would have been challenging each other to a duel and preparing to walk off ten paces.

"It's a big school," I finally said.

Paris shrugged. "I guess."

"We'll probably never see each other."

"You think?" Paris sounded as hopeful as I felt about that.

"And if we do, we duck."

"Okay!" Paris agreed. "So . . ."

So we were out of topics.

Paris walked past me, then stopped. "Hey. Are you dating Tristin?" she asked.

"What? No. No way," I said.

She shifted from one foot to the other. "Do you like him?" she asked.

"Not even a little," I told her.

"Really?"

"Really."

She seemed satisfied by my answer. "Okay," she said, turning to leave again. Then she stopped. "Hey. Nice party." Was she honestly thanking me, or was she mocking me? It was hard to tell.

I decided to accept the compliment graciously, just in case I'd score any manners karma to make up for the night before with my grandmother. "Thanks," I told her.

࿓

I was cutting into my cake that night when the doorbell rang. Sookie had frosted it to look like me—it was so cool. After everyone sang "Happy Birthday" and Mom toasted me, Sookie handed me a knife.

"There's something very strange about hacking into my own head," I said as I sliced through an ear. I was wearing a big pink feather boa around my neck, and I had a "Happy Birthday" paper tiara on my head. The house was packed—practically everyone in Stars Hollow *except* Dean was there.

The doorbell rang for a second and third time.

"Jeez, who the hell's ringing the bell?" Mom yelled. "It's a party! Get your ass in here!"

I looked up just as my grandparents walked in and stood under the arched entryway to the living room.

"Or asses, I guess," Mom muttered under her breath.

I dropped the cake knife and hurried over to them. "Grandma, Grandpa! I can't believe you're here!" I hugged them both. This was so great. "I'm so glad you came. Hey, no tie?" I asked my grandfather.

"I thought I'd mix it up a little." He smiled.

"Grandma, look!" I held up my wrist so that she could see I was wearing the bracelet she'd given me for my birthday. I loved the bracelet because it was from her and she'd picked it out. But as an added bonus, it also lit up when you pressed a button.

"Why, it looks lovely!" Grandma said.

"I want you to meet everyone. Everyone, these are my grandparents!" I said to the crowd.

This was unbelievable, I thought as they started to mingle a little bit. Grandma and Grandpa had never been to our house before. I was so glad they'd accepted my invitation. I knew Mom had had a talk with Grandma after the party, but I didn't know what she said. Whatever it was, it had certainly worked.

After that, the party went by really fast. We had the required time where everyone sat around and told embarrassing stories about me in my youth, ate too much cake, and Miss Patty hit on my Grandpa. All in all, another successful birthday.

As everyone trickled out the door, saying good night, Mom and Sookie started the postparty cleaning ritual. I glanced at my watch—time to meet Dean. I grabbed my brown corduroy jacket and ran outside.

Dean was standing by the hedge, sort of toward the

back of the house, outside the kitchen. "Hey," he said. "Happy birthday." He smiled as I walked over to him.

"Hey," I said. He held out a small box. It was wrapped in newspaper, with a red ribbon tied around it.

"Here you go," he said.

I was really surprised—I hadn't expected a present from him. "You didn't have to get me anything," I said.

"Sorry, that's the rules. You get older, you get a gift."

"I'm sorry about this sort of sneaky thing. I just haven't told my mother yet about you. I mean, not that there's anything to tell. I just—" Am babbling and can't stop.

"That's okay!" Dean interrupted me. "This is better."

He was right. It was better to be standing out here in the moonlight, just the two of us. I unwrapped the gift and lifted the top off the box. Inside was a silver medallion, with a Celtic pattern etched into it. "Oh my God." I looked up at him and smiled. "It's beautiful!" I picked up the medallion, which was tied to a rawhide cord.

"Well, I bought the medallion and then I just cut some leather straps and drilled a hole," Dean explained, sounding nervous. "And . . . well . . . you like it?"

Did I like it? Words could not, would not, describe. "I . . . I . . . it's amazing," I stammered.

He grinned. "Good."

"Thank you," I said.

"Here." Dean took the bracelet and, holding my hand, wrapped the leather strap around my left wrist and tied it together. He couldn't stop smiling, and neither could I.

When he finished fastening the bracelet, Dean laced his fingers through mine and we stood there holding hands for a few minutes, until I realized I'd have to go back inside soon, before my mother launched a birthday/search party. But I didn't want the night to end. I didn't want to say good night to Dean. Something was happening, really happening, between us.

~8

About a week after my birthday, I was walking home from the bus stop after school. As always, I passed Doose's Market. On impulse I decided to go in. I poked my head down a couple of aisles until I saw Dean working on an elaborate can display with Taylor Doose. Taylor is obsessed with decorations. He lives for holidays, new seasons, any excuse to use crinkly paper. Let's just say he could easily have been in the greeting card industry and given Hallmark a run for their money.

"I don't know," Taylor was saying as I walked closer. He eyed the can structure. "It doesn't really look like the *Mayflower*."

It was a bunch of cans of cranberry sauce in a wedge shape, with a sign that said "Autumn Festival" and "Cranberries on Sail, $1.29" hanging above it.

I walked past the display and sort of circled around a couple of aisles, pretending to shop. Dean was wearing his green store apron and he looked really cute.

"Well, we could put a sign on it or something," Dean suggested.

"I don't know. I just don't know." Taylor was clearly perturbed about his ship of cans not working out.

"So, you want to go back to the Plymouth Rock idea?" Dean asked him.

Taylor rearranged one last can. "We'll just live with it that way for a day," he said.

"Okay. Ah . . . sure." Dean said. Out of the corner of my eye, I saw him walking toward me as I stood there reading the side of a cornstarch box.

Dean leaned around the end of the aisle. "You can get two for three bucks."

"Oh. Really?" I asked, looking up at him. "Excellent deal."

"You just had a desperate need for some cornstarch?" he asked.

"Yes. I have very important thickening needs, thank you. Nice apron," I told him.

"Nice uniform," he said.

"Well, you know, I sewed the buttons on with silver thread, so that sets me apart from the crowd," I said, referring to my black pea coat. Everyone at Chilton has to wear the same coat. For some reason my "silver thread" line just killed the conversation. We were totally out of small-talk topics. Feeling awkward, I said, "Well, I guess I should probably get home."

"Wait a sec," Dean said. "You want a pop or something?" He gestured to the back of the store, where the coolers are.

"A *pop*?" I said.

"Give me a break!" Dean said. "In Chicago, they call it pop."

"Well, in Connecticut we call it free soda," I said, smiling. "And, yes, thank you."

I followed him to a cooler with a sliding top. He pulled out two cans and quickly held them behind his back. "All right. Guess what's in each hand and you get the soda."

"Okay, see, the whole concept of a free soda is that it's free. You don't have to work for it," I told him.

He shrugged. "Sorry. You gotta sing for your supper."

"Or your soda." I stared up at him.

"Guess," he said in a soft voice.

"Okay." I thought about it for a second. "In this hand," I said, leaning forward to tap his arm, "you have—"

Before I could say anything, he leaned down and kissed me. On the lips. His hair fell forward and brushed against my cheek and I held my breath the entire time. It was the first time I'd ever been kissed like that.

And then suddenly it was over.

I blinked a couple of times and looked up at him, and he was staring right into my eyes with this happy expression. I was stunned.

"Thank you," I blurted out.

Thank you? Had that just come out of my mouth? I completely panicked and ran out of the market. I didn't know where I was going, but I couldn't stick around Doose's after that.

Cars honked at me as I sprinted across the street, I hopped over pumpkins in the town square and kept running. I pulled open the gate at Lane's house and let myself in through the front door.

"Lane! Lane?" I called.

She came out, wearing an apron and carrying a dishtowel. "What's wrong?" she asked.

"I—I got kissed," I told her. Then I noticed the box of

cornstarch in my hand. "And I shoplifted!" I held up the box.

"Are you *serious*?" She looked even more excited than I felt. "Who kissed you?"

"Dean," I said.

"The new kid?" She was incredulous.

"Yes."

"You got the new kid? Oh my God!" Lane said.

"It happened so fast," I told her, breathless. "I was just standing there—"

"Where?" Lane asked.

"Doose's Market."

"He kissed you in the market?" She was even more impressed by my news.

"Aisle three," I said.

"By the ant spray?" she asked.

"Yes!" I said. How did she know?

"Oh, that's a good aisle," Lane said.

I laughed. "What defines a good aisle?"

"An aisle where you get kissed by the new kid is a good aisle," she said.

I love Lane's ability to just summarize everything into one neat and tidy saying. She's so right.

Suddenly, I got this very clear picture of Dean kissing me, and my legs got all wobbly. "Oh my God. I can't breathe," I told Lane.

"Sit down." Lane grabbed a wooden stool for me.

"I can't sit down. I'm too . . . too . . . oh my God, he kissed me!" I said.

Mrs. Kim magically materialized at my elbow. "Who kissed you?" she asked.

"The Lord, Momma," Lane said.

"Oh. Okay then." Mrs. Kim went off and left us alone again.

"So tell me everything," Lane said, dragging me closer to her. "Play by play."

"So I go into the store, and he offers me a soda, and then he puts two behind his back and tells me to pick one, and then he kissed me!" I explained.

"I'm so jealous!" Lane said. "That's it. I've got to get some dumb, ugly friends!"

"I have to go tell my mom," I realized. I had to tell her right away. I headed through the furniture maze to the door.

"Okay. Call me later!" Lane said.

"Okay." Then it hit me. What was I doing? What was I thinking? I was going to run home and tell Mom when she didn't know anything about Dean except that we had the biggest fight of our lives over this guy not that long ago?

I stopped walking and turned around to face Lane. I was dying to tell Mom about the kiss, but what if it started another fight? "What's wrong?" Lane asked.

"I can't," I said.

"You can't leave?" Lane looked at me as if I were crazy. "It's 'sing your favorite hymn' night at the Kim house. Make a run for it," she said.

"My mom doesn't know about Dean," I told her.

"So? Tell her."

Lane made it sound so easy. "The last time the subject of boys came up, it got very ugly," I reminded her.

"Well, that was different," Lane said. "She thought you were going to quit school over a guy."

"Yes. Over *Dean*."

"Okay, fine. But she doesn't have to know that it was him," Lane argued.

I shook my head. "She'll know."

"How?"

"She'll know. She's Lorelai. What do I do?"

"Well, maybe she'll be more open to the concept now that you're in school and doing so well and everything," Lane said.

"Maybe," I said.

"Try it," Lane urged me.

"Okay. I gotta go." I headed for the door again.

"Hey!" Lane called.

"What?"

"Was it great?" she asked.

I smiled. "It was perfect." At least it seemed perfect to me. I didn't have anything to compare it to, but it felt right.

Except for the saying "thank you" part afterward.

My mother was imitating the refrigerator when I walked into the house fifteen minutes later. She was lying on her back on the floor, with her head halfway into the fridge, making these high-pitched sounds into the telephone.

I stopped and stood there, ready to tell her all about the kiss, and Dean, and how the kiss and Dean went really really well together.

"Yeah, it started last week," she explained to the refrigerator repair shop. "But now it's higher and it's on all the time, so I guess it's growing in confidence. Look, I've already told this to three other people, so is there anyone there who can actually tell me what is wrong with this fridge? No. I am not making the noise for you again. I'm not . . ." And then she started making the "ehhhhhhhh" sound again. I started to lose my confidence. What if we got into another fight?

I took off my backpack and went into my bedroom. I set the pack down and pulled out the box of cornstarch, putting it on my dresser. It looked perfect—albeit stolen—up there.

I went back out to the kitchen with my homework and sat at the table. I looked at Mom and smiled. I wanted to tell her what happened with Dean. I really did. But she was still arguing with the repair shop.

"Here's the deal," she said. "You will send someone out here tomorrow between the hours of eight and nine because I work and I can't wait four hours for one of you guys to show up." She waited a few seconds, then said, "Great. Goodbye." She hung up the phone.

"So, are they coming tomorrow?" I asked hopefully.

"Nope. Monday between three and eight. I am completely useless."

"I'm sorry," I said.

"Oh God, look at this place. It's a sty!" she complained as she got to her feet. "Okay, now I'm crabby. Crabby and useless. Stupid fridge." She kicked it. "Stupid fridge guys. I hate my life!" She stormed out of the kitchen.

A second later, she poked her head back in.

"How was your day?" she said.

I briefly thought about telling her and decided the time wasn't right.

"Oh, fine. Thanks."

"Good," she replied, then disappeared.

It's horrible when the person you're closest to says they hate their life on one of the best days of your life.

∽9

"Okay, just one more time," Lane begged me.

"I've been telling you this story for an hour!" I protested. "It doesn't get dirty."

Lane and I were sitting at the Autumn Festival in the town square, dressed like Pilgrim women. We were wearing black dresses with white shawls around the collar, and actual white bonnets. For the past two years, we had volunteered to man the Cornucopia Can Drive table. People donate cans of food to feed the hungry over the winter, and there's this gigantic Horn of Plenty that gets completely filled with cans every year. "I can't help it," Lane said. "I'm obsessed. I'm totally living vicariously through you."

"Why? *You* got kissed last weekend," I reminded her. "Remember? That guy your parents set you up with. The one who drove the Lincoln Continental. What's his name? Patrick Cho."

"Okay, let's do a little compare and contrast here. You get kissed on the mouth by a cute, cool, sexy guy you really like!" Lane said in a high-pitched voice. Then her tone shifted. "I get kissed on the forehead by a theology major in a Members Only jacket who truly believes that rock music leads to hard drugs," she said.

"Fair enough. You can live through me," I told her. "But just remember that I have *no* idea what I'm doing."

"I'm well aware of that," Lane said. "That's why I've been diligently gathering information for us." She twirled a pen with her fingers.

"What kind of information?" I asked.

"Well, let's see. Dean's from Chicago. Which you know," she said.

"I do."

"He likes Nick Drake, Liz Phair and the Sugarplastic and he's deathly allergic to walnuts," she went on.

"Walnuts bad. Got it." I was glad Dean liked the same music I did.

"Now, he had a girlfriend in Chicago," Lane said.

For some reason this surprised me. "A girlfriend?" I asked. Couldn't he have more allergies, and no ex-girlfriend in Chicago?

"Her name is Beth and they went out for about a year, but they split amicably before he left and now she's dating his cousin, which he doesn't feel too weird about it because he doesn't think they were really in love."

Another really great thing about Lane? She talks so fast that she gets the bad news over with really quickly. "Beth?" I asked.

"I wouldn't worry about it," Lane said, shaking her head.

"How did you get all this information?"

"Through his best friend. Who, by the way, is very cool. So, once you get settled with Dean, do you think you could ask him about Todd?"

"Oh, absolutely." But I couldn't get my mind off the ex.

"Beth, huh?" I asked. "I *hate* the name Beth. It's so . . . *Beth*." Images of a beautiful girl filled my brain. She was laughing and holding Dean's hand and they were kissing.

"Todd *also* said that Dean hasn't been able to talk about anything but you for weeks," Lane said, with a little happy shriek.

Beth who? I smiled and kissed Lane on the forehead, I was so happy.

Lane pulled away from me. "Stop it! You're giving me Patrick Cho flashbacks!"

We both started laughing so hard that Taylor Doose came over and told us that we weren't projecting the right "Cornucopia" image for Stars Hollow. We tried to tell him we were just very happy Pilgrims, but he said that was historically inaccurate.

∾

Then I realized I was totally late meeting Mom so I ran to Luke's.

"Sorry, sorry, sorry," I said as I grabbed the chair across from Mom's.

"Hey, save your apologies for the Indians, missy," she joked.

"People are really in the giving mood today," I said. "The Horn of Plenty is packed."

"That's great." She smiled. "Hey, you want coffee?" she asked.

"Oh no. I'll just take a sip of yours," I said. "I have to get right back."

"Oh, really?" She sounded disappointed. "I thought we were having lunch today."

"I can't. We're one Pilgrim short," I explained. "Sorry. I only have a couple minutes."

"You've been really busy lately," Mom commented. "I mean, we haven't even really talked in a couple of days."

"What do you want to talk about?" I asked. I took another sip of her coffee.

"I don't know. Anything," she said.

"Okay. Well, did you read that article in the newspaper about the polar ice caps melting?" I asked.

But she wasn't interested—at all. "Yeah, yeah, ooh, big deal," she said.

"Fine. *You* pick the subject," I said.

"Great!" Her face completely lit up. "So I was watching *General Hospital* the other day. And you know they have this new Lucky 'cause the old Lucky left to play something where he could have a real name," Mom said. "So anyhow, *old* Lucky had this girlfriend Liz who thought he died in a fire, but then when they got this new Lucky, they brought him back and you were all like, okay, I know it's not the old Lucky and the new Lucky has way more hair gel issues, but still Liz was so upset over his supposed death that you just couldn't wait to see them kiss. You know?"

She stopped to breathe. Huh? "How do you have time to watch *General Hospital*?" I asked her.

"Okay, let's get back to the point here," she said. "What do *you* think about the whole Liz-Lucky kissing thing?"

"I think they're actors being paid to play a part, so it's nice that they're living up to their obligations," I said.

"Hmm," she said, as if she were still mulling it over. "Rory—"

"Look, can we finish this very meaningful conversation later?" I asked. "I promised Lane I'd get right back."

Mom sighed. "Okay. I'll see you later."

"Okay, bye!" I said as I got up to leave and headed back to the Horn of Plenty.

❦

Mom was sitting on the couch with her feet up, reading, when I came home that night.

"Hey, sorry I'm late," I said as I took off my jacket. Lane and I went to her house after our Pilgrim duties were over. Her parents had gone to pick up some antiques from an estate sale in Stonington, so it was one of Lane's few opportunities to play CDs really loud in her room, and she had a lot of new ones she wanted me to hear.

"Oh, hey. No big deal!" Mom called to me. She sounded much happier than she had earlier at Luke's. "There's Chinese in the fridge!" she said.

"Okay!" I went into the kitchen and opened the fridge. I was eyeing the white boxes of leftovers, trying to figure out which one I wanted, when Mom came up behind me and poked her head into the fridge beside mine. "So. Kissed any good boys lately?" she asked.

I practically fell over. She knew? "Who . . ." I asked.

"Mrs. Kim," she responded.

"Of course." I grabbed a box and closed the door. News travels fast in Stars Hollow.

Mom put her palm on the refrigerator door and faced me. "So. He's cute," she said.

"Yeah. He is," I said. How did she know who Dean was, or that he was cute? Oh God. I realized: she had gone to Doose's Market to check him out.

"Can he spell?" she asked.

"He can spell *and* read," I told her. I lifted her arm so

that I could get past her. "How long have you known?" I asked as I opened the cabinet and took out a plate. I was still a little stunned by all this.

"Since this morning," she said. "You didn't think you were going to be able to keep it a secret, did you? You were making out in the market."

"We weren't making out," I said. "It was just one kiss."

"Yeah, well by the time the news reaches Miss Patty's, it'll be a scene from *9½ Weeks*," she remarked.

"So you've known all this time," I said. "At Luke's, here . . ."

"Yeah," she admitted.

"You could've *said* something," I told her.

She put her hands on her hips. "Now, funny, I was going to say the same thing to you," she said.

Suddenly I felt *very* guilty. She was right. I could have told her about Dean and the kiss. I *should* have. I wanted to, but there just hadn't *been* a good time. I looked at Mom, feeling a little awkward. "So."

"So," she said, equally awkward.

"What now?" I asked.

"Now? Nothing." She shrugged.

"No? No lecture about kissing a boy?" I couldn't believe it. Hadn't she completely wigged out when she thought I was quitting Chilton for a guy?

"No lecture. Why? Did you do it wrong?" she asked.

"*No*," I said. I paused for a second. "I don't think."

"I didn't love the way I found out, but you're getting older and these things are bound to happen occasionally," she said calmly. It wasn't what I'd expected. Of course, I don't know what I expected. "Actually, I think it's great," she said, smiling this very wide, semiphony smile.

"No, you don't," I said.

"Yes, I do. I'm thrilled," she said.

"Thrilled."

"Yeah," she said.

"You're completely weirded out by this, aren't you?" I asked.

"No! You're crazy," she said. "I'm perfectly fine with it."

"You don't *seem* fine," I said. "You seem the complete opposite of fine."

"Well, you're projecting that on me because you don't want to think that I'm fine, when I am, as I have said, fine," she insisted.

"Okay." I sat down at the kitchen table and opened the box of food.

"Never been finer," Mom insisted.

"Got it." I stuck the fork into the box and started putting the noodles onto my plate. Mom kept standing there, watching me. "You want some?" I asked, looking up at her.

"No thanks. I'm . . . fine," she said.

∾10

The next night, Mom and I were walking toward Doose's Market to stock up for movie night. No matter what else is going on in our lives, or in the world, we have movie night. So even though things have been a little awkward since we spoke about the kiss, none of that mattered now, because we were united in our love for *Willy Wonka and the Chocolate Factory* and, well, lots of junk food.

However, awkward didn't begin to describe the way I felt now, heading for Doose's—the Scene of the Kiss. Dean was probably in there. This was going to be a possibly great, possibly horrible experience. Mom had never met a guy I liked before, because I'd never really *liked* a guy.

"Okay, we have to be really quick here 'cause the video store's going to close, so stick to our list. No impulse buying, like toothpaste or soap," Mom instructed me as she opened the door to the market.

She was halfway into the store when she realized I

was still standing on the sidewalk, staring at an ad for the Autumn Festival that was posted in the window.

"Rory?" she said, turning around.

"You know what?" I said. "I think we have enough stuff to eat at home."

"Really?" Mom asked, putting her hand on her hip. "Where do *you* live now? Because the home I left this morning had nothing."

"Well, we're ordering pizza," I said. "That's enough!"

"Are you crazy?" she said. "We can't watch *Willy Wonka* without massive amounts of junk food. It's not right. I won't allow it. We're going in." And then she was standing by the market door again, waiting to go in. I, however, was still glued to the sidewalk. "Rory, it's *fine*," she said, coming over to me, knowing what I was feeling.

"It's too weird!" I said.

"I'm going to have to meet him eventually," she said, as if logic would help me right now.

"Okay. How about next year?" I suggested.

She wasn't buying it. "I'm going to be so cool in there, you'll mistake me for Shaft," she said.

"There will be no interrogation," I told her.

"I swear," she promised.

I laid out my list of rules so that she wouldn't embarrass me in front of Dean. "No kissing noises," I said. "No stories from my childhood, and no references to Chicago as 'Chi-town.' No James Dean jokes, no bag boy jokes, no 'father with a shotgun' stares, no Nancy Walker impressions . . ."

"Ah, come on!" she complained.

"Promise me," I begged.

"I really and truly promise," she said. "Now can we *please* go into the market?"

I took a deep breath and let it out, preparing myself.

"Okay. Let's go." I quickly walked into Doose's before I lost my nerve. Once inside, I took a nervous glance around the store. No Dean in sight, after all that. What a relief.

"I don't see him," I told Mom.

"All right. Well, maybe he's on a break." She picked up a basket.

"Yeah. Yeah. Maybe he's on a break," I said, feeling a huge sense of relief. "Okay, so we can shop. Do we want marshmallows?"

"Mm," Mom said, so I dropped a bag into the basket. "And we want jelly beans," she went on, "and chocolate Kisses, cookie dough we have at home . . . and peanut butter. Ooh, do you think they have that thing that's like a sugar stick on one side, and you dip it in the sugar on the other side and then you eat it?"

"We are gonna be *so* sick," I said as we moved on to the next aisle. "It's amazing that we still function." I came around the corner and suddenly I saw Dean. "There he is," I said quickly to Mom.

Dean was filling bags with groceries, laughing and talking to a customer. "Boy, he's tall," Mom said as she stared at him, the basket of junk food dangling on her arm. "That must have been some back bender, that kiss."

"Mom . . ."

"Make sure you warm up next time," she said.

"Okay, we are leaving now," I said, taking her free arm and guiding her toward the front of the store.

"Sorry!" she said in a whisper. "Done now." I let go of her. We were getting close to the checkout lane. "He's got great eyes," she commented. "You gotta love a guy with great eyes."

"Yeah," I said.

"And a nice smile," she added.

"Very nice," I agreed.

"Think we can get him to turn around?" she asked.

Trust Mom to ask about his butt. "It's nice too," I said.

"Really?"

"Trust me," I told her.

We moved up to the conveyor belt and put our collection of calories onto it. Dean looked at me and sort of smiled.

"You girls having another movie night?" the cashier asked us.

"Yeah," Mom said. "It's *Willy Wonka and the Chocolate Factory*."

"Oh, that's nice. Isn't that the one with Gene Hackman?" she asked.

"Um, Gene Wilder," Dean told her.

He can spell, read, *and* toss out movie trivia.

"You're a *Wonka* fan?" Mom asked Dean.

"Um . . . yeah," he said.

Dean was bagging our junk food, so it seemed like as good a time as any. "Um, Dean, this is my mom, Lorelai. Mom, this is Dean."

Mom held out her hand to Dean, and they shook hands. "Nice to meet you, Dean," she said politely.

"Yeah. You too," Dean said.

"Nice apron," Mom added.

"Uh, thanks." Dean looked embarrassed. I was vaguely aware of a dollar total being announced and of my mother handing over money.

I walked toward Dean and he handed me our bag. "Thank you," I said.

"You're welcome." He and I awkwardly looked at each other for a couple of seconds, and then my mom came up.

"So, Dean, nice meeting you," she said. "Hope to see you again."

"Yeah," Dean said.

We headed for the exit. "See? That wasn't so bad," she said quietly.

"You're right," I admitted.

"I said nothing embarrassing, nothing stupid."

"I appreciate that," I said.

"Chill out, Supermarket Slut," she teased.

"See? Even a *little* information in your hands is dangerous," I said. We walked out of Doose's.

"I need coffee," she said.

"Mom, the video store closes in ten minutes!" I said.

"Well, how about *you* run to the video store and *I'll* go get us coffee," she said.

"Fine."

"Go go go!" she said. "Meet you at Luke's!"

I sprinted down the street. I was totally happy, because I got to see Dean, Mom got to see him, *and* it didn't suck. This was all pretty amazing considering we'd started this whole Dean thing off so badly. Everything was okay. I couldn't wait to get home, watch the movie, and lose myself in junk food.

I got the video and headed back to meet Mom. As I rounded the corner, I saw her coming from Doose's Market.

"So?" she asked as she approached me.

"Got it," I said.

"Score. You know, on the one hand, I'm thrilled it was in, but on the other, what kind of world do we live in where no one has rented out *Willy Wonka and the Chocolate Factory*?" she asked.

"Well, *we* rented it," I said.

"Yeah. And thank God for us. Ooh, hey, I invited your friend over to watch it with us," she said.

"What friend?" I asked.

"Dean," she said casually.

"*What*?" I stopped walking and stared at her. Was she insane?

"Yeah." She smiled. "We forgot our Red Vines and he brought them out so I told him what we were doing tonight and he was totally into it so . . ." She slowed down for a second. "Why are you looking at me like that?"

"You invited *Dean*? To our *house*?" I couldn't get my mind around this concept.

"Yes?"

"Are you crazy!" I said.

"Why are you mad?" Mom asked. She really didn't get it—she had no idea.

"Because we haven't even been out on a date by ourselves yet!" I explained. "My first date with Dean is going to be with my *mother*? Are you—what is wrong with you?"

"I'm sorry," she said, sounding genuinely confused. "I thought you would be happy about this."

"In what universe would I be happy? This isn't Amish country. Girls and boys usually date *alone*," I reminded her.

"I didn't think of this as a date," she said. "I thought of it more as a hanging-out kind of session."

"Well, then I don't want our first hanging-out session to be with my *mother* either!" I said. She was the coolest mom in the world, but she was still *my* mom.

Suddenly, she didn't look very happy either. "Okay, stop saying 'mother' like that."

"Like what?" I asked.

"Like there's supposed to be another word after it," she said.

I let out a huge sigh. That wasn't what I meant, and I

knew she probably only did this because she meant well—but it still sucked. "I can't believe you did this! I'm so humiliated." I started wandering down the street toward home. I felt like I was in seventh grade or something—when your best friend tells a boy you like him, so you could find out if he likes you back. I never did that, but I've heard stories.

"You're totally overreacting," Mom said as she followed me down the sidewalk. "I invited him to a movie and pizza—not to Niagara Falls."

I turned around. Why couldn't she understand? "He's the boy that I like!" I said.

"I know. I looked for one that you hated, but it was really short notice," she said lightly.

I didn't laugh. "And now he's forced to come over and sit with me and my mother and eat crap and watch a movie?"

"I just invited a friend of yours to hang out. What's the big deal? I mean, what if Lane had done this?" she argued.

"You're not Lane. You're my mother," I said. "You inviting him is like Grandma inviting a guy *you* liked over."

"You're comparing me to my mother?" Mom asked, horrified by what I said.

"No," I said. "I'm just—"

"I'm Emily Gilmore now." She shook her head. "My, how the mighty have fallen."

"I didn't mean that," I said. I hadn't realized how much that comment would upset her, comparing her to my grandmother.

"I wasn't trying to humiliate you!" Mom said.

"I *know*," I told her. If I could have taken it back, I would have.

"If I was Emily Gilmore, I'd be trying to humiliate you. So, look, I'm sorry," Mom apologized. "I screwed up. I just wanted to—never mind. I'll go uninvite him. I'll tell him it's canceled on account of I just found out that I'm my mother and I need to go into intensive therapy right now," she said.

What? This was not a solution. "No, you can't uninvite him," I said. "He'll think I wigged out or something."

"Fine, then I'll just disappear and leave you guys alone," she said.

"And have it look like I had my mother arrange a date for me? No."

"So, what do we do?" she asked.

There was only one answer. "He has to come," I said.

She nodded in agreement. "Look, it won't be so bad, okay? Just pizza and a movie and hanging out. I promise he won't feel like your mother is there," she said.

"Okay," I said. I didn't see how that was possible, since she'd be sitting on the sofa next to us. But we'd try it. We had to.

Fifteen minutes later, my bed was covered with clothes. I was wearing my pink flowered robe, and my hair was pushed back under a headband. Dean would be there in half an hour and I was not anywhere close to ready.

Mom walked into my room to see how I was coming along. "Hey, this is good. Add some cold cream and some curlers and let him know what he'll be coming home to every night," she teased me.

"This was *supposed* to be a simple night," I said. "Watch a movie, eat junk, go to bed sick, end of story. Now I'm supposed to look pretty and girly, which is completely impossible because I'm gross and I have nothing to wear."

"Want some help?" Mom offered.

"No," I said. Who was I kidding? "Yes," I said.

"Okay, now let's see . . . here." She picked a scarlet-colored shirt out of the pile on my bed. "This is perfect. It says 'Hello, I'm hip and cute, but also relaxed since this is just something I threw on even though I look fantastic in it.'"

I just stared at her in disbelief. "How did you do that?"

"What?" she said.

"I have been staring at that top for twenty minutes. It was just a top. You walk in, and in three seconds, it's an outfit."

"It comes from years of experiencing fashion brain freeze just like the one you had," she said.

"But how do you do it?" I asked.

"What?" she said.

She obviously didn't think it was a big deal at all. "This whole *guy* thing. I mean, I've watched you when you talk to a man," I said. "You have a comeback for everything, you make him laugh, you smile right . . ."

"I smile *right*?" she asked.

"And then you do the little hair flip?" I tried to demonstrate, but it was hard to get it right with my ponytail and headband.

"Twirl," she corrected me, showing me how it was done. "It's a hair twirl."

"And then you walk away and he just stands there amazed, like he can't believe what just happened," I said.

"That's because I just stole his wallet!" she said.

"I'll never be able to do that," I said, sinking onto my bed. "Trig, I can do. Boys, dating, forget it. I'm a total spaz."

Mom picked up the red shirt and sat down at the end of the bed. "Listen. The talking part? You get used to. The hair twirl, I can teach you. The leaving him amazed part—with your brain and killer blue eyes, I'm not worried. You'll do fine. Just give yourself a little time to get there," she said.

"Is half an hour enough?" I asked.

"Plenty. Now come on. Dab on some lip gloss, clear but fruity, maybe a little mascara, wear your hair down and your attitude high." She slapped my thigh as she said that last part.

"You're like a crazy Elsa Klensch," I told her.

"Thank you. Come on now, hustle. We've got a man coming over!"

I jumped up and started putting things away, getting ready for the evening.

∽11

An hour later, Mom and I were sitting on the couch, staring at our table of junk food offerings.

Dean was late.

Dean was almost half an hour late.

No, that wasn't it.

Dean wasn't coming.

I glanced at my watch. This was torture. Pure torture. "What time did you tell him to get here?" I asked Mom again.

"Seven," she said with a nervous smile.

I knew that. But I was hoping she would give me a different answer this time. "Maybe something happened," I said. "Maybe he's not coming."

"Maybe he's just a little late, Miss German Train," Mom teased. She got up and went over to look out the window. Which was exactly what I wanted to do, except that I'd already done it too many times to count. "Oops!" Mom said.

"What?" I looked over my shoulder at her, then jumped up and ran to the window.

Suddenly, I saw what the problem was. Babette, who is very friendly and loves to talk and not necessarily in that order, had snagged Dean on his way in. Dean was standing in the front yard, only steps from our house. He was wearing a leather jacket and looked really incredible. But Babette and her husband, Morey, who was inside and talking to Dean through the window, weren't letting him past. Babette had hooked his arm and Dean was politely standing there listening to her.

"They've got Dean," I said.

"Wait here," Mom said.

I watched as Mom ran outside and surgically separated Dean from Babette. He came up to the door and I let him in, quickly. I took his coat and laid it over the back of a chair.

"I'm sorry I'm late," he said. "I got here like a half hour ago."

I looked up at him and smiled. "We believe you," I said.

Mom, who was coming inside, rubbing her arms from the cold, said, "We'd believe you if you told us you got here three hours ago."

We all sort of laughed. Then there was this deadly silence, where Dean and I should have been talking, but weren't. Thankfully, Mom was a little smoother at this stuff than I was. "So, Dean, how do you like it here in Stars Hollow?" she asked.

"I like it!" he said enthusiastically. "It's quiet, but nice. I like all the trees everywhere."

"Yeah, the trees here are something," Mom agreed. "When Rory was a kid she found out that this one tree was called a weeping willow," Mom went on. "Rory spent hours trying to cheer it up," she said with this big smile. "You know, like telling it jokes and—" I started shaking my head, and giving her a look of desperation. She noticed. "No, I'm sorry. That was me," she continued.

Dean looked very confused.

"So would you like a tour of the house?" Mom quickly asked.

Dean shrugged his shoulders. "Uh . . . okay."

"Well, this is the living room, where we do our living," she said. We all turned around in little steps in a tiny circle to admire the living room. She gestured toward the stairs. "And upstairs is my room and the good bathroom. . . ."

All of a sudden I realized the tour was heading straight toward this very embarrassing collection of photographs of me in various stages. Infancy, toddler-dom, dressed as a pumpkin.

"Mom!" I mouthed, gesturing toward the framed photos. She flipped them over, facedown. She's good. "And uh . . . through here is the kitchen!" Mom said.

Dean walked under the ceiling arch toward the kitchen. I paused beside Mom and whispered, "Thank you."

"You're welcome," she whispered back. Then we caught up with Dean in the kitchen and she continued the tour. "Okay, so your basics. Microwave for popcorn, stove for shoe storage. Refrigerator, completely worthless."

Dean nodded. "Interesting."

The doorbell rang. "I'll get that," Mom said. She put her hand on my shoulder. "Rory, you'll have to take over as tour guide. Make sure and show him the emergency exits."

I got a little nervous when Mom left us alone. "So. That's my mom," I said, glancing at Dean.

"She's got energy," he said.

"Yeah, well, she's ninety percent water, ten percent caffeine," I explained.

Dean laughed, then turned around, looking at the closed door behind him. "So, what's in there?"

"Uh, that's my room," I said.

"Really? Can I see it?"

"Okay. Go ahead." I said.

He opened the door and stepped into my bedroom. "Wow. Very clean."

I leaned against the doorframe and watched Dean check out my room. He picked up my Nick Drake CD. "How much does it suck that they used 'Pink Moon' in a Volkswagen commercial?"

"Oh, I know," I said. Nick Drake was more than a musician, he was a poet. His music is beautiful and I was stunned the first time I saw that commercial. Lane and I still talk about it.

"So . . . you gonna come in?" he asked.

"Oh no," I said. "I've seen it."

"You look like you're glued to the door there," he said.

"No, I'm just observing my room from a new perspective. You know, I hardly ever stand here," I said. "It's making me rethink my throw pillows."

"Would you like me to get out of here?" Dean asked.

"Oh no. I'm fine with you looking around," I said. Sort of.

He picked up my stuffed chicken, which was at the end of my bed. He held it up to his face and said, "Nice chicken."

"Or, you know, at least I *was*," I said.

He laughed, and I realized I was famished. "Mom," I called out, "was that the pizza?"

"Uh, yeah," she responded. We headed back out toward the living room. Mom was standing by the doorway.

"Hey, you hungry?" she said.

"Starving," Dean replied.

"Where's the pizza?" I asked.

"The pizza is . . ." Mom realized she was empty handed. "The pizza . . ." The doorbell rang and Sookie walked in with it. Ah. Very smooth, I thought. Then Sookie introduced herself to Dean.

"Nice to meet you, Dean," Sookie said. "I mean, not that I knew you were Dean, you just look like a Dean," she babbled. "Doesn't he look like a Dean?"

I wanted to die. I think Dean did too. When Sookie finally left we headed for the couch. "I did not invite her," Mom said softly. "I swear."

"Why didn't you just set up a camera in here and broadcast it over the Internet?" I said.

"Because I don't think that big," Mom said.

We walked into the living room. Dean was sitting on the couch, and the pizza was on the coffee table, next to the bowl of marshmallows. "Thank God there's good pizza here," he said.

"Oh yeah. Now we didn't know what you liked on your pizza," Mom told him. "So we got everything."

"Everything's fine," he said.

"Okay, good. So, while it's hot."

We all took a piece of pizza, sat back, and started eating.

∽

About an hour later, we were all sitting on the living room floor watching the movie. "Who needs more?" Mom asked.

"I do." I leaned forward and grabbed one of the few remaining slices of pizza.

"Wow," Dean said. "You can eat."

"Yes, I can," I said proudly. "Wait. That's bad, isn't it?" I asked, thinking of how I was probably not supposed to eat every single thing in front of me.

"No!" Dean said. "Most girls don't eat. It's *good* you eat."

"I'm all for it," Mom chimed in.

I was glad Dean appreciated my appetite, but we'd spent way too much time on this topic already. "Let's talk about something other than my eating, shall we?" I said.

"Ooh — Oompah Loompahs!" Mom cried.

I turned to Dean. "Mom has a thing for the Oompah Loompahs."

"I don't think finding them amusing constitutes having a thing," she said in self-defense.

"No, but having a recurring dream about marrying one does!" I said, and Dean laughed.

Mom wouldn't let me get away with it. "Hey, don't get me started on your Prince Charming crush, okay? At least my obsessions are live. You had a thing for a cartoon."

"Ooh." Dean sounded intrigued. "Prince Charming, huh?" he asked.

"It was a long time ago. And not the *Cinderella* one. The *Sleeping Beauty* one," I protested, slightly embarrassed.

"'Cause he could dance," Dean said, as if he understood. "I've got sisters."

I tried to picture what Dean's sisters would look like. It was good he had sisters. I mean, I'd heard that it was good to meet a guy who had sisters because he'd understand women better. And here was Dean understanding my Prince Charming obsession.

"So, come on, Dean. Tell us one of *your* embarrassing secrets," Mom said.

"Well, I . . . I have no embarrassing secrets," he said.

I didn't believe that, and neither did Mom. "Oh, please," she said.

I sat up a little straighter. "I bet I know one. The theme from *Ice Castles* makes you cry."

"Oh, that's a good one!" Mom said, laughing.

"That's not true!" Dean protested.

"Oh, I've got another one. At the end of *The Way We Were,* you wanted Robert Redford to dump his wife and kid for Barbra Streisand," Mom said.

Dean shook his head. "I've never seen *The Way We Were.*"

"Are you kidding?" I said.

"What are you waiting for?" Mom asked. "Heartache, laughter —"

"Communism," I added.

"All in one neat package!"

Dean looked a little overwhelmed by us. "I'll have to experience that sometime," he said.

"Next movie night," Mom said.

"It's a plan," I said. Mom got to her feet. "I'm going to make popcorn."

"Bring the spray cheese!" I told her as she headed for the kitchen. "So, ah. At what point does the outsider get to suggest a movie for movie night?" Dean asked.

"It depends," I said. "What movie are you thinking of?"

"I don't know." Dean shook some stray strands of hair off of his face. "*Boogie Nights* maybe?" he asked.

I shook my head. "You'll never get it past Lorelai."

"Not a Marky Mark fan?" Dean looked at me and smiled.

"She had a bad reaction to *Magnolia*," I said, and Dean laughed. "She sat there screaming 'I want my life back' and then we got kicked out of the theater. It was actually a pretty entertaining day."

"Yeah?" He moved closer to me.

"Yeah," I said.

"Well, I guess I'll have to come up with a different movie then," Dean said, looking right into my eyes.

"I guess you will," I said.

I turned to watch the movie for a second. This was going *so well* that I was actually afraid. Dean was planning to come back for another movie night—he'd just said that. We'd both agreed on it. That meant he wasn't having an awful time. That meant he liked me.

We laughed and talked for a while, then focused back on Willy.

I changed sitting positions to get more comfortable, and Dean grabbed a pillow from the couch and put it behind my back so I had something to lean against.

"Thanks," I said.

Dean smiled at me, then turned back to the movie. I stared at him a little longer. Suddenly, I realized how alone we were. What was taking Mom so long? Dean turned back to me.

"Hey," he said.

I couldn't take the pressure. "I'll be right back!" I said, bolting to my feet. I needed my mom.

∽12

"Mom!" I walked into the kitchen and put my hands on the table.

"What? What's the matter?" she asked, looking up from the fashion magazine she was reading.

"What are you *doing* in here?" I asked. When you're supposed to be out there making this easier for me?

"Trying to figure out the best bathing suit for my bust size," she said.

"Well, get back in there!" I ordered her.

"Why, what happened? Did the bag boy try something?" she asked, looking concerned.

"No! He's sitting there and he's watching the movie and he's perfect and he smells really good!" I said.

"What?" she asked.

"He smells good, and he looks amazing, and I'm stupid and I said thank you and—"

"Whoa, whoa, whoa. You said thank you?" Mom asked.

"When he kissed me," I explained.

Mom looked totally shocked. "He kissed you? Again? What is he, just out of prison or something?"

"*No*. Not now," I said. "The other day? At the store?"

"Oh, sorry. Strike the prison comment. Okay. So wait. He kissed you? And you said thank you?" It was even more embarrassing when I heard her say it.

"Yes," I admitted.

"Well, that was very polite," she said, smiling.

"No," I said, franticly, "it was stupid. And I don't know what I'm doing here and you're sitting in the kitchen. What kind of chaperone are you?"

"Me?" She held up her hands. "I'm not trying to be a chaperone. I'm trying to be a girlfriend."

"Well, switch gears 'cause I'm freaking out here!" I said.

Mom got this smile on her face. "You really like him, don't you?"

I nodded. "Yeah."

"Well, okay then," she said. "Just calm down."

"I just don't want to do or say anything else that's going to be remotely moronic," I told her. Which meant I shouldn't talk around him anymore.

"Well, I'm afraid when your heart is involved, it all comes out in moron," Mom said.

"Please, come back in!"

"Okay. Let's go," Mom said.

Then it hit me how that would look—that I had gone to fetch Mom, because I was afraid of being alone with Dean. "No, we can't go back in together," I said. "That would be too obvious."

"Okay. I'll go in first, and you . . . go to the bathroom," Mom said.

She literally has a solution for everything. "Okay. Right. Tell him I had to wash my face."

" 'Cause of all the sugar you ate," Mom added, making our story even better. If we had more time, we could get into my motivation for eating sugar and trace it back to my childhood. But the short version would do nicely for now.

"Yes, good. Very good." I pushed Mom back toward the living room.

Then I went into the bathroom and turned on the hot water. I stared in the mirror as steam started billowing up. Is this the face that's hanging out with Dean, about to kiss him again? I shut off the water and headed back to the living room.

∽

After the movie, Dean got up to leave. We headed out and stood on the front porch to say goodbye. "Tell your mom thanks for inviting me," Dean said. We were both leaning against the railing, standing close.

"I'm sorry if this was totally weird," I said. "I mean, with my mom inviting you over and—"

"Hey, no," he interrupted me. "It was good. Really."

"Really?" I asked.

"Yeah," he said.

We looked at each other for a second, and then we both leaned forward and our lips met in this long, very sweet kiss. "Thank you," Dean said in a soft voice. We both sort of laughed, and then he left.

When I went back inside, Mom was already in bed. She was lying on her back, with her arm semi-across her eyes. I scooted onto the bed next to her and lay down, too, putting my head on the pillow.

"So, that went well," she said.

"Yeah. Not bad," I agreed.

"Did I humiliate you?" she asked.

"I don't know." I rubbed my still full stomach for a second. "What did you say to him while I was in the bathroom?"

"That you're pretty," she said with this innocent smile.

"Liar," I said.

"Yeah, well."

"I'm going to go to bed." I sat up and started to leave but couldn't help noticing something was bothering Mom. "Mom? What's the matter?" I asked.

"Nothing," she said.

"Yes, there is," I said. She's such a bad liar. "Come on. Tell me."

"Nothing. I just . . . I really wanted you to tell me about that kiss," she said.

"I'm *so* sorry. I really wanted to, I swear. I just got scared and—"

"I know. I'm not mad. I just wanted to hear about it. That's all. No big deal." She rolled a little on the bed. "It's okay. I'm fine. One too many Caramello bars. Sorry. Okay, you have school. I have work. So. Time for bed."

"Okay. Night," I said.

"Night, hon," she said.

I stopped on my way out the doorway again. "Mom?"

"Yeah?"

"I know this is lame and totally after the fact, but . . ."

She sat up in bed, suddenly looking completely happy and healthy. "Start at the beginning and if you leave anything out, you die!" she said. I sat down on the bed, and she pulled me over toward her so that I was facing her. "Where were you?" she demanded.

"I was in the aisle with the ant spray," I said.

"Ooh, that's a good aisle!"

"I know. That's what Lane said too. But anyhow, he was working and . . ."

It had to have been the ninetieth time I told the story.

Fifty times to Lane.

Thirty-five times to myself.

Four journal entries.

And now I was finally telling Mom, the person I really wished I'd told first.

❧ 13

The next Friday, Mom and I were at my grandparents' house for our weekly dinner, except that my grandfather wasn't there. I missed seeing him—he and I had a closer connection than I had with my grandmother, even though I saw her more often than him.

"Your grandfather called last night and told me to let you know he's bringing you back something very special from Prague," my grandmother said as we started to eat our salads.

"Wow, Prague," I said in admiration. I loved how much my grandfather traveled—he had great stories about all the places he'd been. "How amazing is it that he's going to Prague?"

"It's supposed to be lovely," my grandmother said. "Very dramatic. Castles everywhere."

"Do you know that the cell where Vaclav Havel was held is now a hostel?" I asked. "You can stay there for like fifty dollars a night." I looked at Mom. "Hey, maybe on our big trip to Europe, we can go to Prague and stay in his cell." We were planning this big European vacation for the summer after I graduated from high school.

"Absolutely," Mom said. She was plucking things off her salad plate and shoving them to the side. "And then we can go to Turkey and stay in that place from *Midnight Express*."

My grandmother just stared at her. "Lorelai. What are you doing?"

"Getting rid of the avocado," Mom said.

"Since when do you not like avocado?" Grandma asked her.

"Since the day I said, 'Gross, what is this?' and you said 'Avocado.'"

"I'm focusing on you now," Grandma said to me. "Tell me *all* about the Chilton formal next week."

"There's a formal?" Mom asked.

"How did you know about the formal?" I asked my grandmother.

"Yeah. How did you know about the formal?" Mom asked.

"I read my Chilton newsletter," Grandma said proudly. She's very into Chilton and she's friends with the Chilton headmaster's wife, Bitty Charleston.

"Since when do you get a Chilton newsletter?" Mom asked.

"Well, as a major contributor to Rory's education, I figured I had a right to ask for a newsletter to be sent to my house," Grandma explained.

"Are you serious?" Mom asked.

Grandma went into the den to grab the newsletter. "And it's a good thing too, since obviously you don't read yours," she said when she came back. "*One* of us should be up-to-date on the goings-on at Rory's school."

"Hey, I read my newsletter," Mom said defensively.

"You did?" Grandma asked.

"That's right," Mom said.

Grandma held the newsletter so that Mom couldn't look at it. I felt like I was watching two little kids. "What picture is on the cover?" she asked.

"A picture of a really rich kid," Mom said a little too quickly. She kept picking through her salad. "In plaid," she added.

Grandma turned the newsletter around. "It was a spotted owl."

"In plaid!" Mom repeated.

It was hard not to laugh, but Grandma was taking this very seriously. If I weren't careful, she'd set me up with someone from Chilton for the formal. I wouldn't underestimate her.

"The owls are endangered and Chilton is taking donations to help them." Grandma turned to me and smiled. "You gave a very nice one in case you're interested." She sat back down at the dinner table.

"Mom, don't be giving donations on Rory's behalf!" Mom protested. "I'll do that."

"How can you do that when you don't bother to read the newsletter?" Grandma asked.

"I read the newsletter," Mom insisted.

"You didn't know they were taking donations," Grandma pointed out.

"It's a private school, they're always taking donations," Mom said. "They teach a class in it. I'll get them next time."

"What about the owls?" Grandma asked, looking at her.

"They'll live," Mom said.

"Well, apparently they won't, dear. That's why they need the donations in the first place," Grandma said.

I swear, she and Mom could keep up at this level for hours.

But Mom gave up and turned to me. "So. You've got a formal coming up."

"Yeah." I shrugged. "But I don't think I'm going to go."

"Nonsense," Grandma said. "Of course you're going."

I didn't say anything.

"Mom, if Rory doesn't want to go, she doesn't have to go," Mom said.

"Well, I don't understand why she wouldn't want to go," Grandma said. It seemed like a really good time to exit. "I'm going to get another Coke," I said as I pushed back my chair.

❦

"So, why didn't you mention the dance?" Mom asked as we drove back to Stars Hollow.

"Because I'm not going to the dance," I said.

"Okay. But *why* aren't you going?" she asked.

"Because I hate dances," I said. I watched the little flakes of snow that were drifting around on the windshield.

"Good answer." She nodded, looking at first as if she agreed with me. Then she said, "Except for the fact that you've never actually *been* to a dance."

"So?" I asked.

"So, you really have nothing to compare it to," she said.

"No. But I can imagine it." And imagining me at a formal dance with a bunch of very snobby classmates was not very thrilling.

"Yeah. That's true," she agreed. "But not really, 'cause

since you've never actually been to one, you're basing all your dance opinions on one midnight viewing of *Sixteen Candles*."

"So?" I asked again.

"So, you should at least have a decent reason for hating something before you decide you'll hate it," she argued.

This was funny, coming from her. "Trust me, I'll hate it," I said. "It'll be stuffy and boring, the music will suck, and since none of the kids at school like me, I'll be standing in the back, listening to 98 Degrees, watching Tristin and Paris argue over which one of them gets to make me miserable first."

"Okay, or it'll be all sparkly and exciting, and you'll be standing on the dance floor listening to Tom Waits with some great-looking guy staring at you so hard you don't even notice that Paris and Tristin have just been eaten by bears," Mom said.

This sounded good. Were there grizzlies near Hartford? "What guy?" I asked her.

"Oh, I don't know. Maybe the one who hangs out in our trees all day long, waiting for you to get home?" Mom said.

"Dean does *not* hang out in trees," I told her.

"He bashed his head into a branch last week when I came out of the house too quickly," Mom said.

Picturing Dean bashing his head made me smile. "Why do you care all of a sudden if I go?" I asked Mom.

"I don't care if you go," she said. "I don't want you to miss out on any experience just because you're afraid."

"I'm afraid?" I asked. "Of what?" I stared out the side window.

"Of asking Dean. Of him saying no," Mom said. "Of going to a dance with a bunch of kids that haven't accepted you yet. Of dancing in public," she went on. "Of finding out you should never be dancing in public."

"Okay, okay—I get it!" I had to stop her.

"Listen, I know you are not Miss Party Girl, and I love you for that. But sometimes I wonder—do you not join in because you really don't want to?" she asked. "Or because you're too shy? If the reason you don't want to go is because you really don't want to go, and not because you are in any way afraid, then this is the last time I'll mention it, I promise."

I thought about what she said for a minute. "I don't have a dress," I finally said.

"I could make you one," Mom offered.

"Really?" I asked.

"And we'll buy you some great shoes and some new earrings. We'll get your hair done . . ." She looked really excited about this.

"You won't think I'm an idiot?" I asked.

She wrinkled her nose. "Depends on what hairstyle you choose." She glanced over at me. "This dance could be great for you."

But it was settled. Just like that. I was going to the dance.

Now all I had to do was ask Dean to go with me.

❧14

"He's going to say no."

"Why would he say no?" Lane asked.

"Why would he say *yes*?" I asked back.

We were walking down Main Street on Saturday, and it was about zero degrees out. "Rory, listen to me," Lane said. "There is absolutely no point in having a boyfriend if you can't get him to go to the dance with you."

"He's not my boyfriend," I said.

"Really," she said flatly.

"No."

"Then what is he?" she asked.

"He's my . . . gentleman caller," I said.

"Okay, Blanche," she said, laughing.

"I don't know what he is, but he's not a boyfriend," I insisted. Then again, I wasn't very good at this, having never actually had one before. We'd kissed a few times. We'd watched a movie together. And he'd given me a birthday present that I had yet to take off my wrist.

"Do you think he's my boyfriend?" I asked Lane.

She rubbed her thick wool mittens together. "I think you guys spend a lot of time not kissing other people if this isn't a girlfriend-boyfriend thing."

"Girlfriend," I said.

"You," Lane said.

"Boyfriend," I said.

"Him."

I shook my head. "No, it sounds weird."

"Look, have you had the talk yet?" Lane asked.

"Yes, Lane. Babies come from the stork," I said.

"The *other* talk," she said.

"What other talk?" I asked.

"We've been dating for a few weeks now, where do we stand, what are we to each other, if another girl asks you out, do you feel free to go—"

"How is it that you know so much about this?" I asked.

"Those who can, do. Those who can't, teach," Lane said.

We stopped outside Doose's Market and looked in the window. Dean was at the checkout, just a few feet away from us.

"There he is," Lane stated.

"I should come back later," I said, turning away.

"No, you need to do this now."

"Why?" I asked.

"Because I have to go home soon, and my mom threw our TV out when she caught me watching *V.I.P.* I'm bored and I need some entertainment," Lane said.

"Okay, here I go," I told Lane.

"Good luck," she said. "Oh, and Rory?"

"What?"

"Remember to enunciate," Lane said. "I'm reading lips out here."

I smiled at her and walked into Doose's as Dean was picking up a cardboard box. "Hey," I said.

"Oh, hey!" He smiled. He looked really happy to see me there.

"You're busy," I observed, stalling.

"I just have to put the new green bean shipment on the shelves," Dean said. "Want to help?"

"Yeah. Sure. I love stacking beans." What?

"Okay," he said, as if I were crazy. "Follow me."

Gladly, I thought as I trailed behind Dean. "So, do you work on Saturdays? I forget."

"Well, it depends. Sometimes I come in if I don't have any plans." He set down the box and started to unpack the cans. "Why?"

"No reason," I said. "See, there's this thing at my school next Saturday. Well, it's not really *at* my school, it's given by my school."

"What is it?" Dean asked.

I was off to a great start. Really impressive. "Well, it's this kind of a thing where you go and there's music and you're supposed to get all dressed up and do some kind of dance, and then there's chicken."

"Chicken?" Dean said.

"Well, I don't know if there's chicken, but at these kinds of things they often serve chicken because it's probably cheaper and more people eat it, so actually the logic behind the chicken choice really isn't that bad." I was babbling. If Lane was trying to read my lips now she'd be completely confused—just like Dean was.

"I'm lost," he said with an apologetic smile.

"It's a dance," I told him.

"Ah." He picked up the empty box and walked past me to grab the next box to unpack.

"And it's not like I'm dying to go or anything," I said, "but it is a new school and being a part of the social life is really important at Chilton." What was I doing, quoting out of the school catalog now?

"So. Are you asking me to go to a dance with you?" Dean asked.

"No," I lied. "Yes. I mean, if you *wanted* to go, I would go too."

Dean laughed. "That would probably be good, since it's your school."

"Right. So . . . do you want to go?"

"Honestly?" Dean asked, going for the next box.

"Yeah," I said.

"I've actually never gone to a dance," Dean said.

I was relieved to hear him say that. "Because they're lame?" I questioned.

"Yeah. And it's just not the way I ever wanted to spend my time." Dean turned around and looked at me. "I'm not a big joiner."

"Okay." He was saying no. "Fair enough. More beans, please."

I tried to concentrate on the can-stacking task to hide my disappointment. "You want to go, don't you?" Dean said, coming over beside me.

"No. I don't. I have no desire to go at all," I said. "I was just thinking out loud."

Dean didn't say anything for a few seconds. Then he said, "So, ah, what would I have to wear?"

"What?"

"To this dance," Dean said. "What would I have to wear?"

"Anything you want." I said, brightening up.

"Come on."

"No, really," I insisted. "Whatever you're comfortable with."

"Rory . . ."

"Some sort of pants would be good," I said.

"Rory . . ."

"It's coat and tie," I said.

"Oh man." Dean sighed.

"But you could probably get away with a coat and no tie," I said.

Dean shrugged. "Okay."

"Really?"

"Yeah."

I put my arms around his neck, and kissed him. "Thank you!" I said.

"You're welcome," Dean said, as I turned to leave the store.

Lane was still standing outside, so I gave her the thumbs-up as I walked by the front window. She started bouncing up and down on her heels. When I got outside, we squealed excitedly and walked to Luke's while I told her all about it.

Sometimes I can't help feeling like there's no point doing half this stuff without having Lane to go over it with afterward.

∽

A few days later, tickets for the Chilton Winter Formal went on sale. Tristin was at the table buying his tickets and Paris was in charge, as usual.

"Two, I assume," Paris said.

"You assume, right," Tristin responded.

"So, who are you taking?" Paris asked.

"Why, are you free?" Tristin teased.

This threw Paris and she got flustered. "I'm, uh . . ."

"What am I thinking," Tristin interrupted. "You wouldn't be free this close to the dance." He paid for his tickets and walked down the line to where I was standing, reading *The Group* by Mary McCarthy.

"And she's reading again," Tristin said as he stopped next to me. "How novel."

"Goodbye, Tristin," I said.

"Did you get the novel thing?" he asked. "Because—"

"I said goodbye," I interrupted him.

"What are you doing here?" he asked, not moving on like I hoped he would.

"I like lines," I said, staring at my book.

"The guy is supposed to buy the tickets," Tristin said.

"Really? Does Susan Faludi know about this?" I asked.

He of course had no idea that Susan Faludi was a hard-core feminist who wouldn't tolerate him for even one second. "Unless of course there *is* no guy," he said.

"No. There's a *guy*," I told him.

"A cheap guy," Tristin commented as the line moved forward.

"Well, what can I say? I like 'em cheap," I said. "Sloppy, too. Bald spot. Beer gut. You know, the pants that slip down in the back giving you the good plumber shot? That just sends me through the roof."

Tristin shook his head. "So, who is he?"

"Wow. How many languages can you say none of your business in?" I asked.

But Tristin was still standing there, still following me along in line. "Well, does he go to this school?"

"No, he doesn't." I stared straight ahead.

"Uh huh." Tristin sounded fascinated. "Well, okay, I'll confess something to you. I don't have a date."

"Well, I hear Squeaky Fromme's up for parole soon. You should keep a good thought," I said.

"I actually thought maybe you'd like to go with me," Tristin said.

"You did *not*," I said.

"I did too!" he said.

I glared at him. "You did not, because you are not stupid."

"Why, thank you." He seemed pleased by that.

"Slimy and weaselly, yes," I told him. "But stupid, no. And you'd have to be stupid to think that, given our history, I would ever, barring a safe or a piano falling on my head, want to go anywhere with you. Ever," I added for emphasis.

Tristin blinked a few times. "Okay, fine. I'll take Cissy."

I looked at my book again. "I'll send her a condolence card."

"Yeah. Well, at least she won't be buying her own ticket," he said sarcastically before he walked off.

I stepped up to the ticket table.

"Two, please," I told her, handing her my money.

She looked up at me. "Idiot," she said angrily.

"Excuse me?" I said.

"He's totally nice to you, and you couldn't be a bigger jerk," Paris spat out.

"You like Tristin so much, *you* go out with him," I said.

She didn't have anything to say to that. Instead, she just shook her head. "I don't have change," she said.

"Pay me later," I told her.

"What am I, your Versateller? *Wait* for change." She turned to the guy sitting beside her, who was supposed to be helping her. "I need change! Now!" she barked.

He jumped up and ran off to wherever the change was, completely terrified into serving Paris. "There's no way you're going with someone better than Tristin," she said, looking up at me.

"Whatever," I said.

"You probably don't even *have* a date," Paris said. "You're probably going to come down with some very rare form of flu that only hits losers on dance night."

This was the longest, most annoying ticket purchase I'd ever gone through.

"You know what?" I told her. "I don't want my change. Money makes you shallow." I started to walk away, just as Errand Boy returned with some dollar bills for Paris.

"I've got your change!" Paris yelled. I just kept walking.

∽15

The night of the dance came quickly. "Come on already!" Mom shouted to me as I was getting ready.

"I'm primping!" I yelled back. Actually, I was done primping, and now I was just looking at myself in the mirror.

My dress was this shiny sapphire-blue, and it sat around my shoulders. It was knee-length Ava Gardner mid-Frank Sinatra 1955-cocktail-party-ready. My hair was wrapped up in a bun, and I was wearing a sparkling beaded necklace.

"You're sixteen and you have skin like a baby's ass— there's nothing to primp!" Mom yelled from her spot on the sofa. She'd hurt her back the day before finishing my dress and now it hurt to move. I felt awful leaving her, but there was no way she would let me miss this dance. I'd only be gone a few hours and I'd wait on her hand and foot when I got back. I got up and headed to the living room.

"Okay, okay. Here I come," I told her as I walked out into the living room.

Her mouth literally dropped open when she saw me. "*Wow*. Looks like someone hit you with a pretty stick."

"This dress is amazing," I said, turning a little so that the fabric swirled around my knees. "You've outdone yourself."

"It looks beautiful, babe. You look beautiful," Mom said. "Come here."

"What?" I asked.

"Stray hair," she said.

I went over and perched on the coffee table, and leaned my head toward her. "Fix, please."

"Hmm. I think my favorite part is the shoes." She said, pointing to my black Doc Martens boots.

"The heels hurt," I explained.

"Hey, beauty is pain," she replied.

"I'll just throw them on when I leave," I said.

"You should put them on now and let your feet get really numb," Mom said.

"That's sick," I said.

"Go get me the hair spray," she said.

As I headed back to my room, the doorbell rang and Sookie walked into the house, bringing Mexican takeout food for us. When I came back out with the hair spray, Sookie nearly fell over.

"Oh my God! You're a movie star! I'm serious. At some point tonight, walk down a flight of stairs," she instructed me. "Movie stars always walk down staircases."

Mom held out her hand for the can of hair spray. "Okay, come let me spray you while you try to figure out what she just said."

"*You* don't move," Sookie told Mom. "I got it." She lifted the can of hair spray and pushed the button on top, shooting the spray right into her face. "Agh!" she cried, blinking her eyes quickly.

"Oh no. Are you okay?" I asked.

"Yes, I'm fine. Here, sweetie, hand that to your mother." Sookie held out the can with her eyes closed. "My eyelashes are all stuck together." Then she stumbled off to the kitchen.

Mom had me shield the tacos, and I covered them with a napkin. Then she started to spray my hair. This cloud formed around my head. "God!" I gasped.

"That'll be good for six slow dances, four medium dances, one lambada. But if you plan on moshing, I'd go with one more coat."

"I think I'm good," I said.

In the kitchen, Sookie was doing even more damage to herself, so I rushed in to help her splash water in her eyes until she finally seemed okay. She blinked a couple of times and smiled. I got a paper towel, tucked it in the front of my dress, and got a taco. The doorbell rang and I heard my grandmother come in.

"Rory! Come out here, please," my grandmother called.

"Hey, Grandma," I said as I walked into the living room still eating the taco.

"She has lived with you too long," Grandma said, with this withering look.

"Okay, Rory, lose the bib and the taco, go get your shoes, and come back out and let your grandma take the pretty picture," Mom said.

"Okay," I said. I went back to my bedroom, took off my Docs and paper towel bib, and put on my heels. I did a last-minute check and headed back out to the living room.

"Here she is," Mom said when I entered the room. "Mom, get the camera moving, huh?"

"Oh my. You're gorgeous!" Grandma said when she

saw me. She started taking picture after picture of me. "Smile!" she said. "Oh, I'm so glad you decided to buy her a dress," she told Mom.

I was about to correct her and tell her that Mom had made my dress, when a car horn honked outside. "That's Dean!" I said excitedly.

"Come here, come here!" Mom said. I ran over to kiss her before I left. "Have an amazing time, okay?" she told me.

"I will chronicle the whole evening for you, I promise," I told her. "Bye, Grandma!" I said as I kissed her cheek.

"Where are you going?" she asked.

I turned around. "To the dance."

"You do not go running out the door when a boy honks," Grandma said.

"Mom, it's fine," my mother said.

"It certainly is not fine," Grandma said. "This is not a drive-through. She is not fried chicken."

"Grandma, I told him to honk," I said. "We agreed."

"I don't care *what* you told him," she said. "If he wants to take you out, he will walk up to this door and knock and say good evening and come inside for a moment like any civilized human being would know to do."

"Now, Mom, this is silly. I've met him already," Mom said.

"Well, I haven't. We will wait until he comes to the door," Grandma declared.

"But he doesn't know he's supposed to."

"He'll figure it out," Grandma said calmly. Sure, *she* could be calm.

Dean honked the horn twice more, while I paced around the living room, feeling completely stuck.

"He's not a very bright boy, is he?" Grandma commented. I stopped pacing when I heard footsteps on the stairs outside, clambering up onto the porch. Then the doorbell rang. I raced for the door.

"Don't rush!" Grandma said. "A lady never rushes."

I slowed down. "Hey," I said as I opened the door.

"Hey, I thought I was supposed to honk," Dean said, looking confused.

"I know. I'm sorry," I told him.

"Young man! Come in here, please," Grandma commanded.

I turned around and saw her standing behind me, in the entryway. I cast an apologetic look at Dean as he walked into the house. I love my grandmother, but she could be a bit overbearing at times.

"Hey, Dean," Mom called from the sofa. "Meet my mother, Emily Post."

"Emily Gilmore," Grandma said, staring at Dean.

"Hi," Dean said.

"Hello." Grandma continued her examination.

"Okay, good rap session. You guys are out of here!" Mom said to Dean and me. "Have fun."

"Be home by eleven," Grandma said sternly.

"Twelve," Mom mouthed to me.

"Bye, Grandma. Bye, Mom!" I called.

We were halfway to Hartford when I started to get panicky. What was I doing? It was going to be so awkward and everyone would stare at Dean and me. Paris was probably writing out a list of insults right now. I turned to Dean and said, "Maybe we should just forget about this."

"Okay," Dean said, obviously a little confused.

"I mean, it's just a dance, what's the big deal," I said.

"Beats me," Dean agreed.

"And these kids at my school? Awful. Have you seen *The Outsiders?*" I asked him.

Dean smiled. "Yeah, I have."

"Just call me Pony Boy," I said, and Dean laughed. "I hear this place is beautiful, though. Old and historic. Maybe we could just go in for a minute."

"Fine" Dean agreed.

"Or not," I said. Why was I getting cold feet all of a sudden?

"Fine, too," Dean said.

"I don't know," I said. "Why can't I decide? This is stupid. What do you think?"

"I think that . . ." He glanced over at me. "You look amazing tonight."

I looked over at Dean and smiled. "Well, maybe just a couple of minutes won't hurt," I said.

❧16

I looked around the beautiful ballroom at everyone from Chilton dressed in their formal attire. This was weird. I usually only saw them in uniforms. It was hard to recognize people. I hoped I was sort of incognito myself.

There were dozens and dozens of tables set up, and each one had a little lamp in the middle of a floral centerpiece. There was music playing, and some people were dancing, some people were circulating, and some were just sitting at tables, eating and talking. "Well, it's a very good room," I said as I gazed around the mansion. Dean and I had checked our coats and were standing side by side, looking around the huge room.

"Looks historical," Dean commented.

"I commend the person who suggested this location," I said.

"So, we could just get our picture taken and leave," Dean suggested.

"We could," I agreed a little hesitantly.

"Or we could dance a little first," Dean said, noticing. "I stress—a *little*."

I smiled. "Something slow?"

"That sounds good." Dean took my hand and we headed for the dance floor. On our way, Louise and Madeline intercepted, Louise totally checking out Dean. But Dean took it all in stride and let her know that he was with me and wrapped his arms around me. Louise got bored and she and Madeline headed off.

"I like your dress," Madeline called over her shoulder.

"Thanks." I smiled.

We continued toward the dance floor a second time, when we bumped into Paris and her date.

"I see you came," Paris said, sounding surprised.

"You sold me the ticket," I reminded her.

"I'm Jacob," Paris's date introduced himself.

"Hi. I'm Rory," I said. "This is Dean."

"Excuse us," Paris said. She and Jacob stepped aside as she told him, "Those are *not* friends."

"I was being polite," Jacob said.

"Well, don't," Paris told him.

Dean and I looked at each other. "So, that's Paris," Dean said.

"Yep. That's her," I said.

"She seems fun," Dean commented.

"Oh yeah. She is." We moved onto the dance floor.

"Okay, so this dancing thing is not something I want you to get used to or comment on," Dean said

I put my arms on his shoulders, and wrapped my fingers together behind his neck. "That goes both ways," I said as Dean put his hands on my waist.

We started dancing slowly. "Hey, if I kiss you, is a nun going to come over and boot me out of here?" he asked.

"It's not a Catholic school," I told him.

"So I *can* kiss you."

"Yeah. You can kiss me."

And he did.

"So, Pony Boy, you happy?" Dean asked.

"Yeah. I'm happy," I said, smiling.

∽

We took a break a little bit later. Dean went to get us something to drink, and as I turned around I found myself face to face with Jacob.

"Hi. Rory, right?" he asked.

"Yeah," I said. Was Paris sending her date over to insult me now? What, was she on break?

"Are you having a good time?" Jacob asked me.

"Actually, I am. You?"

"It's okay," Jacob said, looking around the room. "So, was that your boyfriend?"

"Oh, well, I don't know. I'm not sure," I said.

"You're not sure?" Jacob said.

"No. I mean, we've only been going out for a little while, so . . ."

"So there's still some room to play," Jacob said.

Room to play? "What?" I asked.

"Would you like to dance?" Jacob took a step closer to me.

"Oh. No, thanks." I shook my head.

"Maybe I could just get your number," he said.

"For what?" I asked.

"To call you," he said, as if it should be obvious. I didn't get this.

"I'm sorry, aren't you here with Paris?" I asked him.

"Yeah." Jacob nodded.

Did I have to spell it out for him? What kind of guy was he? Even Paris didn't deserve a pseudo-player like this. "So maybe you shouldn't be over here asking me for my number then," I told Jacob.

"Why? Paris is my cousin," he explained with a sheepish laugh.

"Your cousin?" I asked.

"Yeah," he admitted.

"Paris is your cousin," I repeated, just to make sure I heard it right. "You're related." She had the nerve to tell me I wasn't bringing the right date to this dance? She was with her *cousin*.

"Yeah," Jacob admitted.

"Jacob?" I smiled. "It's been very nice to meet you. I hope you have a lovely evening." I turned and walked away to find Dean. So far, this was turning out to be an even better night than I'd imagined.

❦

About half an hour later, Dean and I were sitting at our table taking a break. I had my heels off and my feet were on a chair. I stared at my shoes.

"How could something so pretty be so evil?" I mused.

"How bad is it?" Dean asked.

"It's a pain I've never quite experienced before. I think it signifies my official entry into the club of womanhood."

"That's a rough club," Dean sympathized. "So, you want to maybe go?"

"You're bored," I realized. "Sorry. Yes. Let's go right away."

"I'm not bored," Dean said. "I thought, you know, there's still a little time left, maybe we could get a cup of coffee somewhere . . . hang out a little, take a walk. You know, just us."

I smiled. "That would be nice."

Dean went to grab our coats, and suddenly, Paris materialized at our table.

"So how many people have you told? Four? Five?" she demanded, leaning down so she could interrogate me face to face. "Everybody?"

"What are you talking about?" I asked.

"You know that Jacob is my cousin and now you finally have all the ammunition you ever needed just to pay me back, right?" Paris's voice got louder and louder with every word. She was verging on hysterical.

"I don't *want* to pay you back," I said. "I just want to get away from you."

"Now you can just go all over the school and just tell everyone that Paris Geller couldn't get a date to the dance," Paris said, her voice even louder now. I looked nervously around at the people on the dance floor. "Tell them that she had no one and since she couldn't just not come, she had to get her mother to ask her cousin Jacob to take her and then she had to give him gas money to make him do it!" she said angrily. "Go ahead! Tell them!"

"I don't have to," I said quietly. "You just did."

Paris stood up and turned around. Behind her, about twenty couples were frozen, watching. She pushed through them and ran off.

Despite how she made my life miserable, I still felt bad for her. I wouldn't wish public humiliation on anyone.

Across the room, I saw Dean carrying our coats back toward our table, but then he stopped to talk to someone. *Tristin?* I thought as I watched them. Dean and Tristin talking? That made no sense.

I went over to see what was going on. "Hey. What's going on?" I asked, trying to keep things casual.

"Nothing. Just getting to know your boyfriend here," Tristin said.

"It's going very well," Dean said. "Don't you think?" They were glaring at each other very intensely. I didn't like it at all.

"Oh yeah. We're just about to build a clubhouse," Tristin said.

"Okay. Well, I hate to break up the party, but we should go," I said, looking up at Dean.

"Oh, why? Little girl's got to be home?" Tristin said in a condescending tone.

"*Stop*," Dean said angrily.

"What? I think you two make a very cute couple. Is your horse and buggy parked outside? Gotta get home for the barn raising?" Tristin said to Dean.

I've never seen Dean look so angry. "Let's go," he said, handing me my coat. We started to walk away, but Tristin tried to step between us.

Dean shoved him away. "What the hell do you think you're doing?"

Tristin was completely stunned. "You will *not* push me again!" he said.

"Are you seriously trying to act tough?" Dean asked him. "You're wearing a *tie*, for God's sake!"

Tristin pointed to the exit. "Outside — now."

"I'm *not* fighting you," Dean said. "It'd be like fighting an accountant. I'll call you when I need my taxes done." A crowd started to surround us.

Tristin grabbed the front of Dean's coat and pushed him backward. Dean went in for a punch, and two guys grabbed ahold of his arms. "You don't want to fight me, Tristin!" Dean said.

"Why not?" Tristin yelled, as two other guys struggled to hold him back.

" 'Cause I'll kill you, idiot!" Dean said. He walked past Tristin over to me and said quietly, "Come on, Rory." Behind us, Tristin struggled to get free and came after us. As soon as he got close, Dean turned around. "You will not come near her ever again," he said.

Then we left.

❧17

"That was quite a dance," Dean said as we walked up and over the gazebo, finally back in Stars Hollow. It was a cold night, and my shoes were crunching against the crusty ice and snow. We had gotten some coffee to go, and I was glad I had something hot to drink.

"I seriously don't know what got into him," I said.

"I do," Dean said. "He has a thing for you."

"No he doesn't. It's just a game to him or something," I said.

"He has a thing for you," Dean repeated.

"He does nothing but insult me and make me miserable!" I protested.

"He has a thing for you."

I thought about that for a second. "I don't know how I feel about this whole situation," I said as we crossed the lawn to the sidewalk.

"What do you mean?" Dean asked.

"I don't know. Having my boyfriend defend my honor—it's weird," I said.

"Boyfriend?" Dean said.

"What?"

"You said boyfriend," he said.

"I just meant boyfriend in the sense that the whole defending me thing was very boyfriendy," I said, covering. "But only in the broadest sense of the word, which doesn't even apply at all. Here."

Dean looked at me and smiled. "You are seriously babbling."

"I didn't mean you were my boyfriend," I said.

"Okay," Dean said.

"I don't think you *are* my boyfriend," I said.

Dean shrugged. "Okay." His voice was sort of noncommittal. I couldn't tell if he was insulted or disappointed.

"Dean?" I asked.

"What?"

We walked a few more steps in silence. "Are you my boyfriend?" I finally asked.

"In the broadest sense of the word way?" he said.

"No. In the real 'Hi, this is Dean, my boyfriend' kind of way." So there it was. Out in the open.

"Well, I am if you want me to be," Dean said.

I stopped walking, and he turned around. "I do," I said.

"Okay," he agreed.

"So, it's settled."

"Yes, it is."

"You're my boyfriend," I said.

"That's the consensus."

I couldn't stop smiling as we continued walking down the sidewalk through town. "I'm feeling pretty good about this decision."

"Well, I'm very glad to hear it," Dean said.

We stopped in front of Miss Patty's, the door slightly ajar. It was pretty late—almost ten o'clock. "I guess Miss Patty forgot to lock up," I said.

Dean peered through the doorway. "I've never really seen in here before."

"Then come on in," I said. We walked into the dance studio and Dean checked out all the professional black-and-white photographs on the wall.

"Are all these women really Miss Patty?" he asked.

"Yep. She says she's done everything there is to do in show business except set fire to the hoop the dog jumps through." As I was talking, my purse dropped to the floor with a thud.

"I'll get it," Dean offered. "God, this weighs a ton," he said as he picked it up off the floor. "What do you have in here?"

"I don't know." I took it from him and wandered off around the studio. "A lipstick, a five-dollar bill, gum, hair spray, a book—"

"A book?" Dean asked, following me. "You brought a book to the dance?"

"Yeah," I admitted.

"Thought there'd be a lot of downtime?" he smiled.

"No! I just take a book with me everywhere. It's just habit," I explained.

"So, ah, what are you reading?" he asked.

"*The Portable Dorothy Parker.*"

He took it from me and flipped through the pages, stopping to read one of her poems out loud.

"'There's little in taking or giving, there's little in water or wine; This living this living this living, was never a project of mine.'" He sat down on a beanbag chair. I sat next to him, and he put his arm around me. "Hey," I said.

"What?" he asked, taking his eyes off the book.

"Thank you for tonight," I said. "It was perfect."

"You're welcome." We kissed again, and then we snuggled down into the beanbag chair together, and started to read. It was a perfect night. A little dancing, a little walking, a little Dorothy Parker. Perfect.

∽

"Rory, honey. It's Miss Patty." A voice drifted into my dreams, just as I felt a hand on my waist, shaking me. "Rory? Rory, what are you doing here?"

"Miss Patty?" I said, blinking my way awake. My eyes slowly opened. There was Miss Patty and twenty middle-aged women staring at me. I was still wearing my dress from the dance. I was still lying on a beanbag chair next to Dean. Was this a dream?

"Have you been here all night?" Miss Patty asked.

"I . . . oh no! Dean, get up!" I said.

"What time is it?" he asked sleepily.

"It's five-thirty in the morning," Miss Patty told us.

Mom was going to kill me. "Oh my God. We fell asleep. How could we have fallen asleep?" I asked Dean as I searched for my shoes, my purse, my coat.

"Calm down!" Dean said, getting up. "I'll explain it to your mom."

"Where's my purse? Where's my purse?" I asked.

"I've got it," Dean said "Relax."

"I have to go!" I pushed my way through the crowd of women, racing for the door, not even stopping to put on my shoes—besides I could run faster in my stocking feet on the snow and ice.

"Rory! Wait up!" Dean hurried after me.

"I have to go!"

"I'm going with you!" Dean said. "We'll explain. It'll be okay!"

"No, you *can't* come with me," I said. "You shouldn't be anywhere near my house right now!"

"It's not our fault!" Dean said.

"I know. I just have to get home!" I said. He didn't understand what a big deal this was, he couldn't understand.

He took my arm. "Please let me come with you," he said.

"No!" I said, pulling away.

"Rory!" he called as I sprinted down the street.

"I have to go home!" I shouted.

This time I did run like Flo Jo, my legs moving as fast as they could. The whole way home, I kept imagining how worried Mom must be. She had encouraged me to go to the dance, made my gorgeous dress, and done everything to get me to go. And what do I do? I don't come home. She had to be so upset right now. I hated that she must have been up all night waiting for me, worrying and freaking out.

When I got to our house, it was worse than I'd imagined. My grandmother's car was still parked out front. She must have spent the night. She and Mom were probably up all night wondering where I was. I felt so awful, I was nauseous. I never did stuff like this.

When I crept into the house, through the front door, they were both totally frantic and shouting at each other.

"Look around, Mom! This *is* a life!" Mom was yelling in the kitchen. "It's got a little color in it so it may look unfamiliar to you, but it's a life! And if I hadn't gotten pregnant, I wouldn't have Rory!"

"You *know* that's not what I meant," Grandma said.

"Maybe I was some horrible, uncontrollable child, like you say, but Rory isn't. She's smart and careful and I trust her, and she's going to be fine, and if you can't accept that or believe it, then I don't want you in this house!" Mom shouted.

There was a moment of silence, then Grandma walked out of the kitchen. I pressed myself against the wall so she wouldn't see me on her way out. She slammed the front door behind her.

I slowly walked into the kitchen, where Mom was making coffee. She was standing at the sink with her back to me, filling up the pot with water.

"Mom," I began nervously, "thank you so much for saying all of those nice —"

She whirled around and lashed out at me. "What were you thinking, staying out all night? Are you insane?"

She was so angry at me. She's never yelled at me like that. My eyes immediately filled with tears. "I'm sorry," I said. "It was an accident."

"You're talking to the queen of staying out all night!" she said. "I invented the concept! This is no accident! You can't do this, period!"

"Nothing *happened*!" I said. Why wasn't she listening?

"Do you have *any* idea what it's like to wake up with my mother here, and find out that you never came home?" she demanded.

"So all this is about Grandma being here?" I asked.

"No. This is about the feeling of complete terror when your kid isn't in her bed in the morning!" she yelled.

"I'm *sorry*," I said again.

"And then it's about a different kind of terror when you find out that she's spent the night with some guy!"

"I didn't spend the *night* with him. We fell asleep."

"You are going on the pill," she said, walking away from me.

"What?"

"You are not getting pregnant," she said.

"I'm not sleeping with Dean!" I said.

"Damn it!"

She really didn't believe me. This was crazy! "What happened to all that stuff you said to Grandma? What happened to you trusting me?" I asked. It was hard to talk because I was crying so hard. "You know this was an accident! You're just mad because I screwed up and I did it in front of Grandma and she nailed you for it! Well, I'm sorry. I'm sorry that I screwed up, and I'm sorry that she yelled at you, but *I* didn't do anything! And you know it!" I cried.

I ran to my bedroom and slammed the door shut. I threw my purse and shoes on the floor, then I lay down on my bed and started sobbing into my pillow. How could she not believe me—didn't she *know* me, didn't she *know* I'd never do something so stupid and intentionally hurt her like that?

∾18

A few days went by before Mom and I started talking on a seminormal basis. And that was just to exchange news about our schedules or about being out of half-and-half. I couldn't forgive her for what she'd said. She obviously couldn't forgive me for what I did, or what she thought I did.

It was awful. Christmas is one of our favorite times of the year. The Christmas pageant was in rehearsal and we weren't talking during it, making fun of people like we usually did. I had no one to shop for silly stocking stuffers with. We weren't listening to our favorite bad Christmas songs, or watching Christmas movies we loved and Christmas movies we loved to hate. I was completely out of whack. I even forgot I was supposed to meet Lane that afternoon.

"Hey, I thought we were meeting at Luke's," she said when she found me leaning against the railing of the gazebo.

"We were? Oh God, we were," I said. "I'm so sorry. I forgot."

"Let me guess. You and Lorelai haven't made up yet, huh?" Lane asked.

"Nope. Things are still very *Miracle Worker* in our house. God, how did everything get so screwed up?" I sat down on the bench where I'd left all my shopping bags.

"I think you staying out all night with Dean had something to do with it?" Lane said as she sat next to me.

"And my grandmother being there to witness it didn't help," I added.

"Never does," Lane agreed.

"It sucks," I said. "Things were good. School was good. Dean was good. Now my mother and I are barely speaking, my mom and grandma are barely speaking . . . and Dean's new name is Narcolepsy Boy."

"How's he taking it?" Lane asked.

"I don't know. I haven't seen him since it happened," I said.

"What?" Lane asked. "But that was four *days* ago."

"I know," I said.

"Has he called?" Lane asked.

"I told him not to," I said.

"And he listened?"

I smiled faintly. "No." He kept leaving messages, but I hadn't called him back yet. I didn't want to rile up my mom any more than she already was by actually speaking with the enemy. But I missed him. A lot. I'd bought his Christmas present that afternoon, a copy of *The Metamorphosis* by Franz Kafka. When I told Lane about it, she said she didn't think a book was romantic enough, that it wasn't a good idea. I wasn't sure. I was going to hang on to it for a few days and think about it.

∽

"I wish you'd change your mind!" I called to Mom as I tied the ribbon on our present for my grandmother. I had already gotten dressed for the big annual two-weeks-before-Christmas party at my grandparents' house. I really could not believe that Mom wasn't going. She never missed the Christmas party.

"It's not *my* mind that needs to be changed," she said.

"I don't think she meant it," I said. Mom and Grandma had had another argument, this time about Mom coming to the party, because Mom couldn't make it in time for cocktails. Grandma actually *un*invited her to the Christmas party. I knew it wasn't about the cocktails, though. It was still about the fight they'd had the morning after the dance. It was all my fault, and yet she still wanted *me* at the party.

"Oh, she meant it," Mom said.

"Maybe she thinks she meant it at the time, but I bet she won't mean it later, when I show up there without you," I said.

"And without a map to follow that reasoning, I say take a hat, it's cold outside," Mom said.

"So you just want to hold a grudge," I said.

"Yep. It burns more calories," Mom replied.

"That's not true."

"How do you think your grandma got those legs of hers?" Mom asked. "She's not exactly a StairMaster gal."

"Mom."

"Never saw her on a running track."

"Okay." Sometimes my mother doesn't know when to quit.

"I don't remember the country club organizing a Tae-Bo class," she went on.

"Fine!" I said. "Forget it. Should I put your name on Grandma's present?"

"Yes. Sign it 'the innkeeper formerly known as her daughter.'"

I picked up the present and walked into the living room. "You know what I think? I think you're acting a little immature."

"Hey! I am not acting," Mom said.

"What about the apple tarts?" I asked as I put on my long wool coat. This was crazy, going without Mom. "You wait all year for those apple tarts."

Mom sighed as she got off the couch. "I can live without the apple tarts."

"You've made up songs after eating five of them, with lyrics that contradict that last statement," I reminded her.

She picked up the keys from the bowl on the table by the door. "Oh, you know what? You have to go. You're late."

"You really won't come." I just stared at her.

"What? I'm sorry, did someone say something? It couldn't be Rory. She's already halfway to Hartford."

"Fine, I'll go," I said as I took the keys from her.

"Drive carefully. Watch out for ice!" she called after me. "And bring me back one of those tarts!"

∽

"Come in! You look lovely," Grandma said when she opened the door upon my arrival. She looked great. She was wearing a bright red wool blazer with black fur around the collar and the cuffs, and a black skirt. The house was, as usual, dressed up nicely for the occasion.

"This is from me and Mom," I said as I handed her the gift.

"Well, aren't you thoughtful? Let's put it under the tree," Grandma said.

"Mom actually picked it out," I told her, hoping to smooth things over. She didn't respond as she set the gift under the tree.

"Rory, do you know Holland Prescott?" Grandma asked, completely changing the subject.

"I met her last year," I said.

"Holland! Rory's here," Grandma announced, and we walked into the living room to join her.

Grandpa was standing by the fireplace, talking to one of his friends, Alan Boardman, about business. Grandpa sounded very annoyed. He was holding a drink, but he wasn't drinking it. He was too busy complaining about someone he worked with, calling him a moron.

"Richard, Alan, look who's here," Grandma said.

Mr. Boardman waved, while my grandfather said warmly, "Hello, Rory!"

"Where's your mother?" Alan Boardman asked. "Over by the apple tarts, I assume?"

Before I could say anything, my grandmother piped up. "Lorelai couldn't come tonight," she said.

"She couldn't?" my grandfather asked. He didn't even know she wasn't coming. That surprised me.

"No!" Grandma said cheerfully. "She had to work."

I looked at my grandmother. What was she talking about?

"Speaking of which, I'm going to give that man a call," my grandfather said.

"Richard, you're getting yourself all worked up," Alan warned him.

But my grandfather was determined. He stalked out

of the room. I turned to my grandmother and put my hand on her arm. "Grandma, can I talk to you alone, please?"

"You need something to drink!" she said, slipping into perfect hostess mode and heading for the bar in the other room.

"I want to apologize about the other night," I said.

"Rory, please. This is a party," she said.

"I messed up," I said. "It's my fault."

"This is not the time or place to discuss this," she said briskly. "Your mother should have taught you that."

"Please, don't be mad at her," I begged.

"I'm not mad at anyone!" she insisted, as if this were a foreign concept. "Now go back in and join the party."

"But—"

She handed me a glass. "Take this to Gigi on your way back."

∽

The dinner couldn't be over soon enough for me. My grandfather was upset because he hadn't been able to contact his colleague in London, and he couldn't stop talking about business.

"Is it unbearably hot in here?" Grandpa asked, pulling at his bow tie. His face was getting red, but that seemed normal, given that he was sitting right in front of the fireplace.

"Richard, don't loosen your tie at the dinner table," my grandmother said.

"So Rory, what are your plans for the Christmas holidays?" Holland asked me.

"I'll probably just be hanging out with my mom," I said.

"Oh, it's such a shame she couldn't come—she's always such a kick," Gigi said, and everyone sort of laughed.

"Lorelai wasn't feeling well, so I suggested she stay home," my grandmother said.

This was the second phony excuse she had used. She should get her story straight.

"It's hot in here," Grandpa said, getting up from the table. "I'm going to lower the thermostat." He headed out of the dining room.

"Poor thing, what's wrong with her?" Holland asked.

"I think she has a touch of the flu," my grandmother said. "Richard, forget the thermostat!" she yelled.

"I thought you said she was working," Gigi said, looking at my grandmother with a confused expression.

"Well, she was supposed to work, but then she caught the flu, so one way or another she couldn't have made it," Grandma said quickly. She was a very, very bad liar.

"Tell her we missed her," Gigi said to me.

I smiled at her. "I will."

"Richard! Oh, for heaven's sake. Richard!" Grandma called. She got up from the table and went into the hallway to find him, and then, all of a sudden, we heard this loud shriek.

Everyone sitting at the table looked at one another, then jumped up and rushed into the hallway.

I felt my heart leap into my throat when I saw them. Grandma was crouched next to Grandpa, who was lying flat on his back, on the floor. She was talking to him, but he wasn't answering. His eyes were closed and he was unconscious.

Someone dialed 911 and I stood next to Grandma, looking down at my grandfather, while she patted his cheeks and tried to get him to come to. He looked so

helpless and pale. I'd never seen him like that. I wished
there were something I could do. A thousand scary
thoughts filled my brain. What if my grandfather died
before help came? What if he died—period?

I tried calling Mom at home, but she wasn't there.
Then I tried her cell phone and still got no answer. I was
in such shock over the whole thing that when I got her
voice mail all I could say was, "Grandpa's in the hospital.
Please come!"

The hospital smelled like a combination of school cafete-
ria and floor cleaner. There were beeps and codes and
overhead pages. The loudest of noises, however, was
Grandma yelling at all the nurses, but that did make it
easy for me to locate her when I finally got there.

"Did you find out anything?" I asked.

"Please. They run this place like the CIA," Grandma
complained. A man standing behind the desk, wearing a
trench coat and a scarf, walked up to Grandma and took
her hands. I guessed he must be Grandpa's personal
physician—she'd called him while we were still back at
the house and asked him to meet us at the hospital. "Oh,
Joshua," Grandma said. "Thank God. This place is infu-
riating."

"It's all right, I'm here," he assured her. "I'm going to
check on him right now. Have you filled out the forms
yet?"

"I don't care about the forms," Grandma said. "I want
to see my husband."

"Is she being obstinate?" Joshua asked me.

"Very," I said.

"Let me see what's going on, and we'll take it from

there." Joshua walked down the hallway, into the area marked "Do Not Enter: No Admittance: Authorized Only."

Grandma and I watched him go through the door. She sighed.

"Maybe I should call Mom again," I said. It was awful not having her there. She wouldn't be able to calm down Grandma, but she could probably handle it better than I was.

"Never mind. I'm sure she's very busy," Grandma said quickly as she rifled through her purse for something.

"That's not true!" I protested. I knew she would be there if she'd only gotten the message I left. "I bet she—"

"Rory, go get your grandfather a paper." Grandma pressed some money into my palm.

"But—"

"The *Wall Street Journal* or *Barron's*, whatever they have. He'll want something to read when he gets back to his room."

"Okay. Can I get you anything?" I asked. "Maybe a coffee?"

"No, dear, I'm fine." Grandma smiled at me.

I took off down the hall, searching for a directory so I could find the gift shop. I jumped in an elevator and pressed the button. I was really glad to have a task, something to distract me.

∽

When I came back with the newspapers, Luke was sitting in a chair by the nurses' station. "I gave your mom a ride," he said. "We weren't on a date."

"Oh . . . okay."

He pointed to the "No Admittance" doors. "She and

your grandmother just went back to see if they could find a doctor."

I *knew* Mom would be able to do something I couldn't. "Do Not Enter" signs never stopped her. "Did they find out anything else about Grandpa?" I asked, sitting next to him.

"I don't think so," Luke said. "But give your mom a couple of minutes back there. I bet she finds something out."

"Thanks for bringing her," I told him.

"You're welcome." He nodded. "Hey, you okay?"

My throat sort of closed up. "I don't want him to die."

"Well, you tell him that when you see him," Luke said. "People like to hear that."

Just then the Forbidden Doors swung open and my mom walked out. "Mom!" I said, standing up.

"Hey, you!" She smiled and gave me a big hug. "Hi."

"It was horrible!" I told her. "It happened so fast."

"He's about to come out of the big testing room any minute, so just hang in there," she said. She didn't look worried at all. She seemed really confident that Grandpa would be okay. That made me feel a little better.

"Where's Grandma?" I asked.

"Kicking some patient out of the room with the good view," Mom said.

"Really?"

"I hope they get him unhooked fast, otherwise he's going without the life support machine," Mom replied, only half joking.

"So . . . how long before they bring him back?" I asked.

"Very soon."

"I'd like to do something," I said.

"Like, ah . . . Rollerblade?" Mom asked.

"Like get some coffee or make phone calls or do *something* that isn't standing here waiting," I said.

"Okay, got it." She nodded. "Well, as partial as I am to the phone, I'm voting for the get coffee idea."

"Okay. Good. Luke? Tea?" I offered.

"Peppermint preferably," he said.

"I'll be right back." I started to walk away.

"Hey," Mom said, coming after me. When I turned around, she said softly, "He's going to be fine."

"I was just getting to know him," I said.

"I know."

"I don't want him to —"

"He's *not*," she interrupted me, before I could say it. "Now go get my coffee."

The coffee machine was jammed, so I returned coffeeless. I did find chicken soup and Pez. I swear, it's what was there.

While I was gone, they had brought grandpa down to his room.

As soon as he woke up, I read some of the latest news to him from the *Financial Times* and the *Wall Street Journal.* It seemed to make him feel better, and I liked keeping him company. When Grandma returned with fresh new pillows, she asked me to finish reading to him later so she could speak with him privately.

As I got up to leave, I leaned closer to Grandpa. "If I hug you, is it going to hurt?" I asked.

"Pain is a part of life," he replied.

I gave him a quick hug and kissed him gently on the cheek.

"This little girl likes you," Grandma said as she put her arm around my shoulder.

"Well . . . she has good taste," Grandpa said, and he smiled. That's when I knew he was going to be all right.

When I went out into the hallway, Luke was sitting in

a chair just outside the room. He had his elbows on his knees, and he was staring at the floor. He looked very pale and a little distraught.

"Where's Mom?" I asked.

"Looking for coffee," he said in a monotone voice.

"What are you doing?" I asked.

"Staring at my shoes."

"Okay," I said. "Carry on."

In the visitors' lounge, Mom was repeatedly pressing the coffee button on the hot-beverage machine. Coffee still was not coming out.

"No luck?" I asked.

"I think I'm wearing it down," she said, pushing another button.

"You're pathetic," I said.

"Is the doctor back?" she asked.

"Not yet."

"So." She gave up on the hot-drinks machine and turned to face me. "You had a visitor tonight."

"Yeah? Who?" I asked.

"Narcolepsy Boy."

"Dean came over?" I asked.

"Oh, yeah," Mom said as she wandered past me, moving on to the change machine. "He pulled the old tapping on the window bit."

"Were you mean?" I asked.

"Excuse me! I am never mean," she said.

"You were mean," I said.

She sort of smiled, looking a little nicer. "He told me nothing happened."

"Nothing *did*," I said.

"I know," she said.

"You do?" I asked. "Really?"

"Rory, there are only two things that I totally trust in

this entire world," Mom said. "The fact that I will never be able to understand *what* Charo is saying, no matter how long she lives in this country, and you."

"Hopefully not in that order," I said.

"You just have to understand the major panic factor that went on there," Mom said.

"I do," I said. "I really do. And I'm so sorry. Nothing like that will ever happen again, I swear."

"Don't swear," she warned me.

"Why not?"

"Because you are your mother's daughter," she said.

"What does that mean?" I asked.

"It means that things can happen. Even when you don't really mean for them to happen."

"They will *not* happen," I promised.

She gave a half laugh. "Okay."

We didn't say anything for a second.

"I hated going to that party tonight without you," I told her.

"I hated you going to that party tonight without me," she said. "How were the apple tarts?"

"Oh, Grandma didn't make them this year," I said. We gave up on the coffee machine and started walking out of the lounge, back toward Grandpa's room.

"Really? That's weird," Mom commented.

"Oh, I know," I said.

"Hmm. Are you lying?" she asked.

"Through my teeth," I said.

She put her arm around my shoulder. "Good girl."

∽

A little bit later, Joshua gathered us all together in Grandpa's room and said that Grandpa had a "touch of angina." It meant he had to change his diet and exercise more, but if he did that, he would be okay.

I was so incredibly relieved and happy. Grandpa was going to be fine—he'd actually get to go home in the morning. Mom didn't hate me anymore. And Dean had come over to see me.

Mom wanted to stay at the hospital with her parents for a while, so she asked Luke to give me a ride home. She told me to go call Dean and "talk mushy" to him and argue over who got to hang up first. She can be such a freak sometimes.

But after Luke dropped me off at home, I did go inside and call Dean. I woke him up, and we talked for about two hours. Nothing too mushy. Honest.